REFLECTIONS

Featuring stories and poems by:
J.A. Cummings
Sassa Brown
Katie Jaarsveld
Alanna Robertson-Webb
Kally Jo Surbeck
Bob Byrne
Drew Starling
Julianna Rowe
C.L. Williams
C. Marry Hultman
Luna Black
Shashi Kadapa

Published by Irish Horse Productions, 2020

Reflections

© 2020 Irish Horse Productions

Cover Art © 2020 CJ Graphics & Design
Published by Irish Horse Productions
Edited by Sassa Brown

Table of Contents

Marjorie's Mirrors

J.A. Cummings

When her adopted mother passes away, Cynthia inherits
more than she ever expected.

Cynthia still couldn't wrap her head around it. The call had come in the middle of the night, waking her from a sound sleep and melding with the dream that still had a hold on her half-asleep brain. It took until the middle of the next morning to realize that it was true, and that Marjorie Evans was dead.

Marjorie had been Cynthia's best friend when she was a child, their seventy-year age gap notwithstanding. The lonely little girl had found a place of welcome in her next-door neighbor's home. Cynthia's mother often entertained gentlemen callers and locked her child outside, rain or shine, and Marjorie had brought her inside. She'd fed her when her mother forgot and gave her a place to sleep when the door stayed locked for days on end. She taught her how to play the piano and how to knit. She'd taught Cynthia about caring for others, a lesson she never would have learned at home.

When Cynthia grew up and went away to school, she and Marjorie had stayed in touch. In fact, when holidays came and the dormitory closed, it was to Marjorie's house that she returned. Her mother moved away at some point during her sophomore year, never providing a forwarding address, but Cynthia didn't really mind. She had her mother in the house next door.

Now, Marjorie was gone, and Cynthia's heart was breaking. She sometimes caught herself hoping that it wasn't true, trying to believe that it was part of the dream the sheriff's call had shattered, but she had to face the fact. The only person who had ever loved her was gone.

They said it was a cardiac arrest, and that Marjorie had died peacefully in her sleep. Cynthia was grateful that her ending had been as gentle as dying could be. Marjorie deserved nothing less.

Marjorie had been as lonely as Cynthia, a 79-year-old widow who'd never had a child. She was as alone in the world as that little girl had been, and the fact that they had found each other had been a blessing in a world of turbulence. As she walked into the lawyer's office to discuss Marjorie's estate, Cynthia silently gave thanks for Marjorie's presence in her life.

The secretary greeted her at the door, then ushered her into a small conference room at the back of the office. She was given a bottle of water and was left alone. The table had a vase of real flowers and a china cup filled with complimentary pens bearing the logo and name of Stanley Tulin Elder Law. She had nearly finished her water by the time the attorney came in.

"Miss Lewis? I'm Caroline Miller, Mr. Tulin's associate."

Cynthia looked up to see a perfectly coiffed brunette, her slim form dressed in a chic suit and high-heeled pumps, holding a thick manila folder in her hand. She shook hands with the attorney, who sat down across the table from her.

"First of all, please let me extend my condolences on the death of your loved one."

Cynthia smiled politely. "Thank you. She was a wonderful woman."

"I'm sorry I never had the pleasure of meeting her, although Mr. Tulin visited her in her home several times in the process of setting up her estate and trust accounts."

"I had no idea she had done all that. She never told me."

Miller smiled brightly. "Then you're going to be receiving a number of surprises today. I hope you're prepared."

Cynthia's palms started to sweat. "That sounds ominous."

The attorney opened the folder and started laying out piles of paper-clipped documents. "Mrs. Evans was a very organized person. She had several assets, which have all been bequeathed to you."

Her heart nearly stopped. "To me?"

Miller nodded. She continued to lay out paperwork. "Her bank account, including her investments. The investments and accounts she inherited from her late husband, which have been accruing interest for forty years. Her cabin in Northern Michigan, and her house here in Farmington."

"You're kidding."

"Miss Lewis, I never kid about estate business. This is all legit." She pointed out the places where Cynthia needed to sign, and it seemed to take forever to get all of the paperwork finished. When she had finally signed all of the documents in triplicate, the lawyer nodded.

"Excellent. I'll have these notarized, and the deed will be sent back here. You can pick it up, or we can mail it to you."

"I'll pick it up. I don't trust the mail." She put her hand to her forehead. "I really can't believe this is happening."

"Mrs. Evans wanted to make certain that you were taken care of."

Cynthia blinked away tears. "She always did."

"She also wanted to be certain that you received this."

The attorney handed her a sealed letter. The envelope was cream-colored stationery with tiny hand-painted lilacs, and Cynthia recognized it immediately. She had given that set to Marjorie last Christmas. The envelope had been closed with sealing wax, and an embossed angel was set into the hardened red blob. On the front, in Marjorie's shaky hand, were the words, 'Open only after I am dead.'

She pressed the letter to her heart and blinked away a tear, overwhelmed by her adopted mother's generosity, still hurting from the loss.

"Thank you," she told the attorney. "I appreciate everything."

Miller smiled. "Do you have a key to the house?"

"Yes." She wiped at her eyes. "Yes, I've had one for years."

The two women stood, and they shook hands across the table. "I'll be in touch when the deed arrives, and I'll let you know when the money is deposited into the account."

"I don't care about the money, but..." She shook her head. "I can't believe what she's done for me."

"She must have loved you very much."

"She did. She certainly did."

The attorney walked her to the exit, and she went to sit in her car and cry tears of grief and gratitude.

****

Cynthia parked in Marjorie's driveway, flanked by the flowerbeds that were still blooming, evidence of the careful attention her friend had bestowed upon them. Lilies of the valley, irises, and peonies stood out in splashes of vivid color against the white siding of the little house, and she remembered many springs planting flowers at Marjorie's side. She sighed and left the car and she stepped on the same paving stone with the chipped corner that always rocked beneath her feet. It was all so familiar, so well-known… and yet all so different.

She went to the concrete steps that led to the back door. A red, terracotta flowerpot stood on the stoop, overflowing with a glorious bleeding heart bush. She remembered telling Marjorie that her green thumb went all the way to the shoulder, and Cynthia wished that her friend - her mother if love were to decide relationships - were still there to be told again.

The screen door squeaked the same off-key song she remembered, and the key slipped into the knob as easily as ever. She turned the key and pushed open the door, stepping into the mudroom. Still air from the interior of the house rushed out at her, and it carried the scent of Marjorie's lavender soap, and for a moment, it was almost like her friend was there to welcome her home with a loving embrace. Cynthia sank to her knees, overwhelmed by grief all over again, and leaned against the door jamb to weep.

She had known Marjorie was old, just as she'd known that all human lives were finite. It had been a concept, but not a reality. Cynthia hadn't been ready to lose her and was blindsided by the fact of her friend's mortality. It was too soon, and she still needed Marjorie's steady comfort and wise counsel.

I'm only eighteen, she thought desperately. How am I going to own a house? Pay the taxes? What am I going to do? Behind her, the house her mother owned glowered at her over Marjorie's split-rail fence.

Cynthia refused to look at it. She had seen those darkened windows glaring at her like angry strangers, and she didn't need to see them again. She didn't even look to see if her mother was home. The only mother she'd ever really had was Marjorie, and now she was gone.

When her tears subsided, she stood and closed the door. The mudroom was really a glorified landing, one step leading up into the kitchen on one side, ten steps leading down in the basement on the other. She knew this house like the back of her hand and could have drawn the floorplan in her sleep. It was hard to believe that it was hers, now.

No. This house would always belong to Marjorie. She walked through the tiny kitchen, passing the magnets on the refrigerator proclaiming Bible verses and emergency phone numbers, and stepped into the little dining room.

The sideboard was covered with Marjorie's collection of twelve china teacups and saucers, each one decorated for a different month of the year. It had been a mission of sorts that the two of them had pursued together, gathering those cups from eBay and online stores until they were able to get a finished set. The last cup and saucer set they'd needed to complete Marjorie's collection had been the one for March.

Cynthia held the cup and looked at the little painted gold shamrocks on the green china, remembering Marjorie's delight when she'd opened her 89th birthday present and found it sitting in the box. There had been good times. So many good times.

She went into the living room and sat in Marjorie's easy chair. It still smelled like her Aspercreme and the other pain-killing ointments that she would rub into her arthritic shoulder.

Cynthia pulled the letter out of her purse and opened it carefully, trying to break the seal without destroying the angel in the wax. The letter said:

My dearest Cynthia,

If you are reading this, then I have gone to my Heavenly rest. Do not weep for me, for I am happy. I am reunited with my Oscar and we are together now. I hope that you will live happily and well until we can meet once more.

The house and everything in it, and the cabin and everything in it, and my bank accounts and car and everything I owned is yours now. You are the daughter I never had, and it gives me peace to know that you will want for nothing. There is only one thing that I ask of you.

When you go to the cabin, please leave the mirrors covered.

With all my love and in certainty that we shall meet again,
Marjorie

It was a small, albeit strange, request. She had never known Marjorie to be superstitious in any way, but now that she thought about it, she remembered the one time she'd gone with Marjorie to the cabin in Grayling for the summer months. There were two bedrooms, both with antique dressers crowned with built-in mirrors, the kind that rotated end over end. Both of those dressers and the mirrors they held were draped with sheets, and at no time were those sheets removed.

She'd thought it odd at the time, but she'd been young, and the lake was nearby and there were woods to explore, so she'd let it go. It was something that needed a little investigation, and she resolved to go up north at her first opportunity to check things out.

****

On the first clear weekend she had, one that fell in the gap between two semesters at college, Cynthia loaded up her car and headed north. Grayling was a tiny little town that straddled I-75 in the northern half of Michigan's Lower Peninsula. It was a sliver of a rustic small town in what Cynthia had heard people call "God's Country." The cabin was northwest of the town, situated on a long dirt road and surrounded by red pines.

It had clearly been a long time since anyone had been at the cabin. Its yard was overgrown, the grass easily to the middle of her thigh as she waded through it on the way to the door. The hinges were rusty, as was the wire on the screen door. Dead flies lay piled between the screen door and the wood of the main door, and she kicked them out of the way with a disdainful nudge of her hiking boots. The key turned, but the doorknob stuck, and she had to use her shoulder to get inside.

Nothing a little oil wouldn't fix.

Inside, dust was thick on everything, but in a sort of blessing, all of the furniture had been covered with sheets the last time the cabin had been closed. She went through the motions of opening the cabin for occupancy, getting the water flowing and checking that the electricity was still working. She removed the sheets and swept the floor, and she was surprised to find that the vacuum still functioned.

There was no dishwasher, but there never had been, and she was relieved that the plumbing had its act together. The bedrooms were on the upper floor, two rooms on opposite ends of the cabin. She went up the stairs and cleaned off the years' worth of dust she found there, as well.

When the cabin was clean enough to live in, she returned to the bedroom that had been hers ten years ago when she'd last stayed there. Cynthia stared at the dresser for a long time, and while she had come here specifically to examine the mirrors and see why they needed to stay covered, she couldn't bring herself to ignore Marjorie's last request. She left the sheet over the mirror and, tired from all the cleaning and the five-hour drive to get to Grayling, she went to bed.

****

Cynthia was awakened from a sound sleep when the night was still dark. Something was scratching in the wall beside her head. She groaned and slapped the wood with her hand. The noises stopped, and she rolled over, content that she had scared away whatever rodent had been there. She was almost asleep when she heard the scratching again, this time from another wall. Cynthia sat up and rubbed her eyes in irritation.

This time, the sound was coming from the wall behind the sheet-covered dresser. In the moonlight through the window, the drape-covered furniture looked eerie and unsettling, and she felt a chill that had nothing to do with the air in the room. The scratching was louder than before, more insistent, and as she watched, the mirror beneath the sheet began to move.

Slowly and deliberately, it tipped toward her, rotating on its metal pins. The sheet slid down its surface, displaced by the slow and purposeful spinning. Cynthia's heart pounded in her throat while the mirror continued to spin, completing a complete revolution and ridding itself of its covering in the process. The glass faced the wall now, away from any of the moonlight, and yet a faint blue glow shone around the edges, illuminating the wall behind the dresser like a brilliant shadow.

Cynthia rose from her bed and crept toward the dresser, knowing that she should just leave but needing to know what was happening. She grasped the mirror's top edge and pulled down.

It spun around and clicked into place far more quickly than her tentative tug should have allowed. The mirror glass glowed blue-white, and clouds like a hurricane whirled over what should have been a reflective surface. At the heart of the miniature hurricane, she could see a dark spot, a spot that grew larger as she watched. Cynthia stepped back, her hand flailing out as she tried to find something to use in self-defense, but she found nothing but the bedclothes.

The spot was now human-shaped, and as she stared, a foot extended from the mirror, followed by a leg. She tried to retreat further, but her legs were jelly and she fell. She found herself sitting on the floor, too terrified to move and unable to speak. The foot and leg were joined by a torso, and then a man in a black 1930's suit stepped out of the mirror and into the room.

He was tall and gaunt, and his suit hung on him like he was a scarecrow. His hands were skeletal, with fingers that were far too long, and his gangly arms and legs were spider-like.

The worst part was his face, which had no features at all. It was only a blank white expanse with no nose, no mouth, and no eyes. Still, despite all that his face was lacking, Cynthia knew that the specter was staring at her with rage.

A voice spoke in her head. -Marjorie.-

It was too much. Cynthia found her voice with a pitiful cry and fainted.

****

When she woke, the sun was bright, and she was lying in her bed, the covers pulled up to her chin. Cynthia stared at the wall, disoriented. Slowly, afraid to see but knowing she had to anyway, she sat up and looked toward the dresser. The sheet was in its place, and there was no sign of any faceless man or unnatural light.

"It was a dream," she whispered aloud. She pressed her hands to her head and laughed at herself. "Of course, it was a dream. How stupid."

To prove to herself that nothing had happened, she climbed out of bed and went to the dresser. With a quick mental apology to Marjorie, she grabbed the fabric and pulled it away from the mirror, exposing the silvered glass to the light.

It was just a mirror, cloudy with age and with chipped edges by the frame. There was nothing strange or remarkable about the thing at all, and Cynthia laughed at herself for her fear. She touched the glass, and it was cool against her fingertips but there was nothing else of note.

"Just a mirror," she whispered. "Just a mirror."

The back of the mirror was just as unremarkable, and she shook her head at her own foolishness. The fatigue and stress of dealing with Marjorie's death were working on her, and she decided it was good that she had come up to the cabin after all. She clearly needed a vacation.

Cynthia showered and dressed. She had no food in the cabin, so the power of hunger compelled her to get in the car and drive back toward town. She decided she was too lazy to cook, so she opted to pull in at a little diner with a 1950s-style sign. The place was called Peggy's, and it looked like the sweet, harmless kind of place that Marjorie would have loved.

Her meal was pleasant and uneventful, and she spent most of it scrolling through Facebook and Instagram on her phone. Nobody bothered her, she had a good breakfast, and the dream of the mirror faded into a distant and unpleasant memory.

She stopped off at the store to buy supplies for the cabin and headed back. When she went through the door, the air had a heavy feeling, as if she had just intruded into an ongoing argument and was standing between the glaring combatants. The weather outside was hot and muggy, but inside the cabin, it was cold enough to make her shiver. She grabbed her jacket, a light windbreaker she hadn't expected to need, and pulled it on over her T-shirt.

There was still one room she hadn't cleaned, and she had to face it. Steeling herself to the task, Cynthia climbed the stairs and headed into Marjorie's room. It was easier than going into her house had been because there was no scent to remind her of the woman she had lost.

The room was neat but dusty, and a mirrored dresser, the twin of the one in her room, stood beneath a sheet of its own. Cynthia brought the vacuum cleaner in and got rid of the dust on the floor. She pulled off the bedclothes to wash off the years of neglect, and as she passed the dresser, she hesitated.

A thought insinuated itself into her mind, almost as if someone else was thinking it. She had taken the sheet off the other mirror, and even if it was back in place now, wasn't it really too late? Hadn't she already completely violated Marjorie's dying wish? She hated to admit it, but she had, and anyway, it seemed silly now in the light of day to be afraid of something so fragile.

She reached out to slowly and deliberately pull the sheet away. An envelope was tucked into the mirror, its edge pushed in between the frame and the glass. It had her name on it in Marjorie's handwriting, a stronger and firmer version than that on the letter she'd been given by the lawyer. Cynthia dumped the laundry onto the floor and pulled the envelope free. It wasn't sealed, and she pulled out the letter it contained.

Cynthia,

I knew you'd take the sheets off the mirrors even though I told you not to. You were a curious child, and the woman you've become is just the same. I'm not angry, or I wouldn't be if I were there.

Your curiosity has made you a Mirror Guardian, whether you want to be one or not. My own snoopy nature caught me in the same trap when I was your age.

There is someone who can tell you what you have to do now. His name is Martin, and you can find him if you ask for him at Harding Pines Park. The park ranger will summon him for you.

I'm sorry you did this but not entirely. You will make a good Guardian, and I knew you would replace me the moment that I met you. We were destined to meet, and I want you to know that I could not have loved you more if I had borne you myself.

Be brave, Cynthia. You will need all your strength to do this task that has been set before you. I know that you can do it. I've always known. Call for Martin. He will help you.

With all my love,
Marjorie

Cynthia stared at the letter and re-read it twice. The words sounded like a mad woman's raving, but Marjorie had never been anything but practical and sane. Her palms began to sweat, and she wondered if the dream from the night before had been no dream at all. Needing to know more but afraid of what she'd learn, she abandoned the sheets where she'd dropped them and headed to Harding Pines.

Harding Pines was a state park named for a local World War One hero, a man who had been essentially forgotten by the rest of the world. The park was a dense stand of old-growth forest with walking paths, something that had been preserved virtually untouched by man.

Cynthia and Marjorie had come here many times during the summer they'd spent at the cabin, and from her child's perspective, she had been convinced the trees were the tallest in the world. She doubted that they would still seem as huge.

The park entrance was easy to find with a large wooden sign pointing the way inside. The guard shack where someone was supposed to be checking vehicles for state park entrance passes stood silent and empty. The road was narrow with towering trees on all sides, and though there was a slight breeze, the forest greeted her with an expectant hush.

There was a small parking lot beside a wooden building, a visitor center that housed a ranger station and a museum dedicated to Patrick Harding, the man for whom the park was named. Hers was the only car, which seemed strange on such a beautiful summer's day. When she went inside, the museum section of the building was deserted. She walked past the display of Harding's uniform and medals and knocked on the ranger station's door.

It took a moment, but eventually, a white-haired man with wire-rimmed glasses opened the door. He was dressed in a ranger's uniform, but he hardly looked the part. He looked more like a befuddled professor.

"Good afternoon, miss," he greeted. "How can I help you?"

Cynthia felt suddenly foolish and embarrassed. "I, uh…I'm looking for someone named Martin."

The man hesitated, clearly surprised by her request. He raised his bushy white eyebrows. "Who told you to ask for him?"

"It was in a letter from Marjorie Evans."

"Marjorie…" He sighed. "So, I guess she's gone?"

Cynthia nodded. "She passed away last month. I'm sorry."

He bowed his head for a moment, and she wondered if he was praying. Finally, he looked up at her. "I'm Rupert Green. I'll call Martin for you. Please wait out here."

Green closed the door without waiting for her to respond. The day was getting weirder by the minute. Cynthia wandered back out into the museum and stood, looking at the exhibits.

The interpretive cards for the displays were old, typed with an old manual typewriter that dropped its R's below the text line. The cards were yellowed with age, their edges soft. There was no dust, but she felt strongly that nobody had touched this place since the 1940s. A strange smell filtered out of the ranger's office, something like burning leaves and incense, and she saw a light flash under the door. Alarmed, she went to the office and knocked.

"Mr. Green?" she called. "Mr. Green, are you all right?"

The door opened, and she was startled by the appearance of a handsome young man in a black suit, a black turtleneck in place of the usual shirt and tie. His hair was black as well, wavy but neat, and his eyes were the palest blue she had ever seen. There was something otherworldly about him, and in the air around him was the faintest whiff of sulfur.

"Miss Lewis?" He offered her his perfectly manicured hand. "I'm Martin. You sent for me?"

She hadn't told them her name. Her instincts told her not to take his hand, so she ignored the offer and backed away. The man stood and smiled at her, charming and easy on the eyes, but everything about him made her nervous.

"What's the matter, Miss Lewis?" he asked. "You look like you've seen a ghost."

"Maybe I have." She backed up another step.

"I assure you. You have nothing to fear. Just take my hand, and I will explain everything to you."

Cynthia's nerves were telling her to run. "No... I..." Realization filled her mind, along with unexpected words, and she straightened. "Is this a test?"

He didn't answer. He only grinned.

She knew what to do, but she didn't know where that knowledge had come from. She only knew what she had to say.

"Get thee behind me, Satan."

The handsome man's grin faded, then turned into a sneer. He vanished in a flash of black smoke, and Cynthia gasped, stumbling backward. The stench of sulfur lingered, but it was joined now by the scent of roses. As the smoke cleared, the old ranger stepped out of the office.

"Sorry for that, but I needed to be sure of you," he said. "Martin will be here in a few minutes."

She flashed with anger. "Needed to be sure of me how?"

"I wanted to be sure you had the ability to sense evil and to not be fooled by it." He smiled apologetically. "I didn't mean any offense. It's just that what you're being asked to do can't be entrusted to someone without a good feel for things."

The door to the building opened, and a blast of cold air rushed into the room. It smelled and felt like snow, and Cynthia turned in surprise. Another man entered, wearing a blue suit and a long black raincoat. He was young, with a pleasant yet serious face, and as soon as she saw him, she felt a rush of comfort and security. He smiled and walked forward.

"Rupert," he greeted. The two men shook hands, then embraced like old friends. "So good to see you again."

"Martin," the ranger greeted, grinning. "It's been... what? Forty years?"

"Almost."

"That's impossible," Cynthia interrupted. "You're not even forty years old."

Her head was pounding, and she put her hands to her temples. Nothing made sense anymore, and she was wondering if she even knew what was real.

Martin turned to her and spoke in a smooth, reassuring voice. "This must be very difficult for you. I'm sure you have many questions."

She looked up into his friendly face, and all of her fear melted away. She had never encountered anyone who radiated so much goodness.

"I have nothing but questions," she admitted. "I'm so confused."

Martin nodded. "Please, let's sit down over here. You look like you could use a seat."

The three of them walked to a trio of benches near the fireplace in the visitor center. Martin sat beside her, and Rupert sat on the bench across from them. She looked at the two men, waiting for them to speak.

"I understand if you have questions. I also understand if you have too little information to even formulate any questions right now. So, let me start with a question of my own. Have you uncovered the mirrors?"

She wanted to lie, to avoid getting in trouble for doing such a thoughtless and impulsive thing, but she told the truth. "Yes."

Martin nodded sagely while Rupert pinched the bridge of his nose. She wanted to sink into the floor and disappear.

"No, no. That's all right," Martin told her. "It's human nature to be curious. We understand that you would want to know why those mirrors needed to remain covered, and Marjorie understood that, too. We aren't angry with you for uncovering them... just a bit saddened."

"Why disappointed?" she asked. She kept her voice hushed as if she was talking in a church or standing on sacred ground.

"Disappointed because now you must learn that the world is more than you thought it was but in pleasant ways." Martin smiled sadly. "Did she tell you in her letter that you would be a Mirror Guardian?"

Her head ached. "Yes. Why... how did you know she left a letter?"

"I know many things. And I am far older than forty years, and so is Rupert." He turned on the bench and held out his hand to her. Without thinking, Cynthia took it.

As soon as her skin touched Martin's, she felt a surge of energy from the contact, lancing up through her hand and up her arm like lightning. The sensation was startling but not painful, but she still gasped when the power reached her head.

She heard sounds in her mind like metal doors striking against wooden walls, and with each bang, her senses reeled. She felt her mind like a living, physical thing, and it was larger than her skull, almost too large for the building. Each bang made her mind feel bigger, and she shook her head against the hallucination.

"Don't fight," Martin's soft voice advised. "This is necessary."

Cynthia's mind shuddered again, and she gasped, "What are you doing to me?"

"Preparing the way."

She squeezed her eyes shut, but even so, she saw. She could see the earth as a globe that she was spinning in her hands, covered with a tracery of glowing lines. The lines intersected and sent tiny branchlets in all directions, like neurons in an injured brain. She felt like she was diving through space, flying down at an impossibly fast speed toward one glowing node where the lines had converged.

"What...?"

"Hold on," Martin coached her. "See it through."

Cynthia splashed into the glowing energy as if it was water, and she was suddenly swept along in the flow, carried by yellow-white rivers of power. She struggled against it, terrified, but no harm came to her. She didn't drown, and she didn't suffocate. She was uninjured in all of the ways that mattered, but still, she was almost too afraid to breathe. Nothing could have prepared her for this.

The energy stream that she was riding on deposited her on solid ground that was covered with pine needles, the soil rich and loamy. Though her body was motionless on the bench in the visitor's center, in her mind she stood up and planted her feet into the earth. The cabin was before her, and in the upstairs windows, a green light was shining.

"I have to go up there," she whispered out loud.

"Yes. You do."

"What do I do?" Cynthia asked. Her voice was distant, a hollow whisper, and it sounded strange to her own ears. It echoed inside the vastness of her consciousness.

"Go up the stairs," Martin told her. "I will be with you."

She went into the cabin, walking through the door just like a ghost, and suddenly she was in the bedroom where she had slept the night before. The faceless man was there, crouching in the corner, hunched down so his knees were near his ears and his hands were clawing at the floor. He snarled at her, though he made no sound.

"Tell it to go back." Martin was standing behind her in the room, his suit and raincoat traded for gleaming white robes. Huge wings with pearlescent feathers beat slowly behind him, growing from his back and reaching nearly to the ceiling.

"You're an angel."

"Tell it to go back."

Cynthia turned to face the creature in the corner. "Go back where you came from!"

"By what power do you send it?"

"By my power!"

"Who owns this home?" Martin prompted.

"I own this home!"

The faceless man hissed again, then leaped through the mirror to the dimension it had come from on the other side. A sheet appeared in mid-air, and she grabbed it before it could fall to the ground. With two quick strides, she went to the dresser and threw the sheet over the mirror, covering it completely.

She drew a symbol on the cloth, holding it tight against the glass as she did. Cynthia didn't know the symbol, but it felt like she knew what to do. She didn't hesitate or overthink. She just did it.

"Now," Martin said. "The other room."

She thought of the other bedroom, and then she was there, standing before the other mirror. She was starting to understand that in this astral state, traveling was more thought than motion. She didn't know why all of this made sense, even when it made no sense at all.

The mirror was throbbing with green light, and from the edges of the glass, sickly white tentacles were extending out, reaching toward the wooden supports that held the mirror on its pegs. Martin appeared behind her again in his angelic finery, and she found the words to say.

"No. You can't be here." She pointed at the mirror and the creature that was trying to come through it into the world. "Get back where you belong! This is not your home!"

"Who owns this home?" Martin asked.

"I own this home!"

The creature in the mirror roared, and the walls shook with the sound of it. The dresser rocked on its wooden legs. A snapping sound filled the air, and then the mirror cracked, releasing a spray of tiny fragments into the room. Martin held up his hand, and the splinters of glass fell to the floor, inert. Another sheet appeared, and Cynthia caught it, covering the dresser and drawing the sigil like before.

The house made a sound like a sigh, and then she was back in the visitor center, clutching Martin's hands. Rupert sat quietly, chewing on an unlit pipe. She looked at the two men, confused and disoriented as if she was waking from a deep sleep. She stared at Martin.

"You're an angel," she said. He nodded. "And Rupert?"

"Another guardian. The portal he watches is in the woods."

Cynthia had a million questions, but she could only put one into words. "Is this real?"

"Sadly," Martin nodded again. "Yes."

She released her hold on his hands, and he let her go. Shaken, she scooted a little farther away from him, sliding down the bench.

"There's much you need to learn," Martin told her, "but you have time. Your duty as a Mirror Guardian is to prevent demons from using those mirrors as doorways into the material world. You see, they want to escape the misery of the Dark Plane, and they also want to destroy those who are allowed to live free of it. They are destroyers, and they bring ruin to everything they touch."

Cynthia rose and paced, trying to will her hands to stop shaking. "But… are these the only mirrors that I have to guard?"

Rupert nodded and finally spoke. "Yes. The glass in those mirrors was formed with demonic power. Those mirrors cannot be uncovered now that you have sealed them with your power. I would suggest keeping them here in the cabin, where nobody will find or disrupt them."

"Leave them here?" she asked, incredulous. "But anybody could find them, just walk in and do whatever…"

"There are few places where the power of a ley line intersection is powerful enough to contain them. This is one. There is another place known to you, as well."

She looked at the old man, then at the angel. "The house in Farmington?"

Martin nodded.

Cynthia put her hands to her head. "How do I know this? How did I know that symbol? What is it, even? I don't… I'm not cut out for this. I can't be."

"You are, or you wouldn't be able to do it," Rupert pointed out. "Trust the Spirit. It will never guide you wrong."

"You've sealed the mirrors appropriately," Martin told her. "And as long as they remain covered, all will be well."

She knew that he was her mentor and that he knew more than she did on the subject. She also knew that she respectfully disagreed.

"I'm not leaving them here," she told them. "I have a better idea."

****

It took a few extra hours to make the trip since she had to bind the sheets to the mirrors and keep checking that the sigils hadn't slipped, but finally, she reached the house she had inherited from Marjorie. Cynthia moved the mirrors down into the basement and, working long into the night while following the things that her subconscious drove her to do, buried them deep beneath the foundations.

When the last shovel full of dirt had been replaced and the ground had been stamped down so smoothly that there was no sign of digging left, Cynthia leaned wearily on the wall.

"Well, Marjorie... I covered your mirrors."

Someday, her own replacement would arrive, drawn to her door the way she had been drawn to Marjorie. Until then, she would wait. And she would watch.

The End

About the Author

J. A. Cummings was born in Flint, Michigan, and was raised in a nearby town called Clio. Appropriately enough for someone growing up in a place named for the Muse of history, she developed a passion for reading and the past that continues to this day. Her love of poetry and storytelling quickly followed.

Her life has been one of numerous false starts, unexpected endings, and fascinating side trips that lasted far too long. All of that chaos has informed her writing and improved her understanding of what it means to be human, both the sorrow and the glory.

She still resides in Michigan and also writes as Tiegan Clyne.

Something is Wrong with My Reflection
Alanna Robertson-Webb

What happens when you combine Hawaiian folklore, an old mirror, and a bottle of Nyquil? Something strange, that's for sure. The narrator finds this out the hard way after purchasing a mirror from a thrift shop. Since then, strange things start to occur in their apartment.

Do you ever get the feeling that, when you look in the mirror, your reflection doesn't quite follow you? Sometimes it seems to lag by just a fraction of a second, and it's so subtle that it's almost impossible to perceive it.

I noticed.

Last Friday, I woke up to the 6 a.m. screeching of my alarm clock, and I was groggy because I had downed several tablespoons of Nyquil the previous night in a feeble attempt to stave off a bad head cold. Through half-lidded eyes I brushed my teeth and got dressed, but when I was in front of my closet mirror. I observed something strange: no matter what I did my reflection moved just a heartbeat after me. I squinted at myself, convinced that the Nyquil and lack of sleep were messing with me.

That, or I reasoned that the mirror was just old and starting to warp a bit. A week ago, I had gotten the silver-framed looking glass from an antique store, which is called the Tin Can Mailman. The hand-painted hibiscus flowers swirling around the edge of the frame reminded me of the flowers my grandmother used to grow, and I bought the mirror out of sheer impulse. I live in Nuuanu, Hawaii, and the little old lady running the store swore up and down that it was crafted by one of the *Menehune* themselves.

Stories of the mythical dwarf tricksters abound on our island, so I just smiled, nodded, and bought the mirror. My grandmother had also told me about the little pranksters, and it just seemed like the mirror was meant to be with me.

After fooling around with my reflection for a few more minutes I took one last look at myself and shrugged, opting to go about my day per usual, and within minutes I had forgotten all about my strange experience. At work, I didn't really ever see my reflection, and it was all I could do to get through my day without falling asleep. By the time I entered the last of my data onto my Excel sheet I was exhausted, and I nearly got into a car accident when I dozed off at the wheel for a moment. I vaguely remember locking my apartment door behind me, and then I flopped down on my couch and passed out.

The sound of shattering glass woke me. I lifted my head, my muscles feeling weak, and I tried to peer around the room. I couldn't tell where the sound had come from, and my chest tightened painfully as my heart beat at a too-rapid pace. I couldn't make out any sounds in the apartment other than the faint hum of my radiator, and there was no illumination except for a few distant streetlights that crept through my blinds. My phone had died long ago, which I figured was probably for the best since a bright light would have been a beacon to the intruder.

As I raised myself off the couch, I tried to catch any signs of movement but didn't see anything out of place. I had nothing to defend myself with, but with the kitchen being so close I figured I would be able to grab something useful, even if it was a frying pan.

My body trembled as I pushed off the couch, and as silently as I could I slid off my flip-flops. I stealthily made my way to the kitchen, though I nearly tripped over the metal strip that divided the living room from the kitchen. As I wrapped my fingers around the handle of the frigid, cast-iron frying pan I began to feel a little silly. I had no reason to believe that anything other than a super-vivid dream had woken me, yet I was creeping around my apartment like I was going to bash some skulls in. I nearly sat the pan back down, but I hesitated.

My gut still said something was wrong.

I tightened my grip on the handle, tiptoeing my way slowly across the tiles to the hallway. At the end of the corridor, I could see both my bedroom and bathroom doors, and they were opened just as I had left them. I couldn't see any shadows in the doorways, and I still couldn't hear anything, so I proceeded forward.

Everything was fine. Nothing was out of place, and my two tiny, fourth-story bedroom windows weren't shattered or tampered with as far as I could tell. I didn't have a bathroom window, and the mirror in there was perfectly intact. I felt like a fool, but as I leaned against the hallway wall I exhaled a shaky sigh of relief that I wasn't being robbed or assaulted. The only thing even remotely out of place was a long, narrow crack that ran the full length of my closet mirror, which I was sure hadn't been there that morning. That alone wouldn't have been enough to make the shattering noise that I heard though, so after quadruple checking that the windows were locked, I willed myself to label it as part of a dream.

I fell asleep quickly, despite the gut-churning, predator-esque feeling that something was still wrong. The next week passed uneventfully, except for the moments when my reflection would be distorted. Each day the crack was spreading outwards like a spiderweb, and my reflection began to look more and more misshapen. My ears looked too pointed, my eyes looked too black, my nose looked too hooked and my nails looked like curved claws in the distorted fragments.

Two nights ago, I couldn't take it anymore.

I unhinged the heavy, old-fashioned mirror, nearly dropping it on my feet in the process. It weighed too much for me to carry it, so I dragged it down to the elevator outside my apartment door. Since Halloween was coming up, I put a 'FREE FUNHOUSE MIRROR' sticky note on it and sent it down to the first floor. I figured that it would make a fun addition to one of the annual haunted attractions that my neighborhood ran, or at least the first person who wanted it could take it. I knew our building didn't have any security cameras, so I wasn't worried about the security staff trying to bring it back to me.

I slept peacefully that night, my rest uninterrupted and nightmare-free. I woke up yesterday feeling a little bit better, and after I blearily drank my way through two cups of coffee, I dragged myself to my closet. I had just finished buttoning up my shirt when I realized my reflection was pointing at me.

That's weird. The mirror has to be warped...

I didn't have time to finish my thought as a cold, chest-squeezing wave of panic crashed through me.

How was the mirror back here?

No one had been in my apartment, and I sure as anything wasn't the one who had hung it back up. The thing in the mirror that looked like me was laughing so hard that it seemed to be wheezing, its shoulders shaking silently as its ribs pressed grotesquely against its heaving sides. My jaw went slack, and I could feel my mouth drying out as fear caused my hands to start shaking. Without thinking I blindly began feeling around with my left hand, my eyes never leaving the mirror, and I soon grasped the thick anthology that I had been searching for.

I threw the book as hard as I could at the mirror, the jangling crunch of shattering glass an echo of the sound I had heard the night I thought there was an intruder. Everything would have been fine if the pieces of glass didn't have a tiny hand reaching out of them. In the span of mere seconds, a creature about the size of a small child was standing in front of me. I think I passed out from shock for a few minutes because when I opened my eyes next, the little being was crouching near me, a concerned expression on their bearded face.

"Oh, goody; you not dead!"

I was thinking that I very well could be.

"Hey, you, up up. You okay now!"

The little humanoid gave me a gentle prod in my shoulder, and I twitched away from the creature.

"Who, wait, what do you want?"

"Hehe! I is yours now."

"Mine?"

"Yes yes! Very own Menehune!"

The excitable little person began rocking himself back and forth on the soles of his feet, the motion so rapid that he almost appeared to be bouncing. I couldn't fathom what

I was seeing, and the temptation to just close my eyes again was strong. Just as I did, I felt his little hand, this time on my foot. He whapped my slipper, the vibration coursing up my leg, and I had to resist the urge to kick out at this strange little person. I had to be hallucinating, and I wasn't going to play into my own delusions.

Then he yanked my slipper off and began mercilessly tickling my foot.

"Hey, stop it! Oh, hahahahaha! Stoooop!"

"Is revenge! You not very good for tricking, no no, so I tickle instead of trick. You get too scared, try to throw mirror away. That bad! You no be upset, just happy with me."

"Well, if you didn't play creepy tricks then I wouldn't be upset! I also wouldn't be talking to myself right now, so clearly this is me having a mental breakdown. Work and being sick have gotten to me, and I'm just going a little crazy. That's all!"

My voice cracked. I could feel hysteria clawing its way out of me as I spoke, and like a damn breaking it finally spewed out on my last word. My chest was constricting, and I could feel my heart beating much too rapidly as my short breaths stumbled out one after another. I got myself up, marched unseeingly to my bed and promptly laid down, my eyes fixated firmly on the green paint on my wall. That paint was fascinating, and calming, and it didn't have a bug-eyed little man staring at me.

It was perfect.

For the briefest moment I had myself convinced that things were normal, and that I just needed to lay here for a bit until I felt stable again.

Then he spoke.

"Heya, hey! You okay? Look pretty bad, yeah."

Fine, I guess I was going to have a conversation with my delusion. Why not? I was clearly nuts, so I may as well take it all the way.

"I'm super-duper-ultra fabulous! Thank you for your concern."

My sarcasm could have melted a hole through a metal door, but I didn't care. At least I didn't, until I saw a very sad-looking face rise up over the edge of my bed. The little man looked like he was about to cry, and for just a moment I felt my heart soften. At least my delusions couldn't really hurt me, right? I sighed, reaching over to pat a spot on the comforter near the edge. He eagerly scrambled up, his stubby legs faster than I would have expected, and he plunked down on my bed with a sigh.

"This better than mirror. I try to make breaking sound to get you to let me out, but you no get hints good, huh?"

One question down, a million more to go.

"Nah, I'm no good at hints. So, if you could make noise this whole time then why didn't you just talk to me?"

"No can do, breaks the rules."

"Rules?"

"Yeah, human-Menehune talking rules. We have to be hush-hush to be okay, or else humans do nasty experiments to us."

"Why are you here then, if it's such a big risk?"

"You own mirror, I live in mirror. You got me out of mirror, so we friends now. Simple simple!"

"No, it's not simple! We aren't friends, and you can crawl right back in that mirror for all I care!"

I half expected him to be wounded, to see a look of betrayal cross his bearded face, but instead he just smiled gently at me and patted my foot.

"Silly human, friendship you will learn. I go clean up broken mirror now, then make home in bathroom mirror."

He was off the bed before I could respond, and I heard him plod across the floor as he hummed a tune I didn't recognize. Great, I was going to have an uninvited roommate who wouldn't even pay rent. I might as well check myself into a nut house now. Maybe with the right dose of the correct medication the being would go away, or at least I wouldn't have to think about him living in my bathroom. Oh damn, he was planning on living in my bathroom...

"Wait, the bathroom is where I shower! Ahhh! You can't fricking live in there!"

About the Author

Alanna Robertson-Webb is a New York author who enjoys long weekends of LARPing, is terrified of sharks and finds immense fun in being the chief editor at Eerie River Publishing.

She lives with a fiancée and two cats, all of whom like to take over her favorite cozy blanket when they think they can get away with it. She is currently an MRO support member by day, and an editor and author by candlelight.

While she has been published before, which is wonderful, she one day aspires to run her own nerd-themed restaurant.

Her work can be found here:
https://arwauthor.wixsite.com/arwauthor
and here:
Alanna Robertson-Webb.

Reflection

Kally Jo Surbeck

Rationalize. Reflect. Recap. Repeat. Remember. Reveal.
Residual. Renew. Real.
Expectation. Emotion. Evasion. Emotion. Excuses.
Emotions. Evolving.
Feeling. Frustration. Fears. Fixation. Finality. Fatality.
Focus. Friends. Family.
Lore. Legends. Life. Like. Lust. Longing. Love. Loss.
Lies. Live.
Experience. Exceptions. Excavation. Evaluation.
Extension.
Conceive. Create. Care. Crave. Connive. Convolute.
Confess. Cooperate.
Tension. Trouble. Toss and Turn. Tremble. Tears. Take.
Toughen. Triumph.
International. Interstate. Industry. Introspection. Irritate.
Irate. Innovate.
Operate. Oversee. Ominous. Obfuscate. Opinion.
Obliterate Oppression.
No New Noise Now. Near Next Nexus.

About the Author

Internationally Bestselling, multi-award-winning author Kally Jo Surbeck can be found on Facebook, Instagram, or her webpage here: www.kallyjo.com

There You Are
Drew Starling

A mysterious tale from an anonymous guide on the
journey of life and death.

You wake up, but you can't see anything. You search for your senses, but you can't feel anything. Your body is gone. Your world is gone. Everything is gone. But you're definitely awake. You're alive. You know you are. What were you doing before this? Were you asleep? Does it matter? It doesn't matter. You're awake and you can't see or feel a thing and it doesn't feel good.

Wait.

It doesn't *feel* good. Are you sure? Very. That's something! That makes you *feel* a little better. So, you can feel insofar as you can think. 'I think therefore I am.' Who said that? Shakespeare, right?

Where is this *feeling* coming from? It has to come from somewhere. Last time you checked you had a head, a heart, lungs, and a nose, and - and wow, for some reason that all seemed so long ago. Like maybe it never happened at all. Maybe you've always been this way, and what you're *feeling* now is (and was) actually your prevailing state.

Well, let's just *say* you did have those things– a head, a nose, etc.– where would these feelings be coming from? Your brain. Right. So, you have a brain. Or do you? Let's just *say* you do. And if we're going to *say* you have a brain, then what else can we *say* you have? (It already feels like you want to make leaps here. Watch it.) Why are you allowed to have a brain and nothing else? Because you *felt* something there.

Ah.

So, what else can you feel? Can you walk? Nope. Come on, the answer is right in front of you. Are you even listening to me?

Oh, you are. Good! You can *hear* me. So then does that mean you have ears? Yes. It does. Let's say you do. What else can you *hear*? What about *that*? Can you hear it? Can you? Yes, you *can* hear that slow, distant dripping sound. It's faint, but it's there. Just like you! Where is it? It sounds far away. Think about that for a second.

Far away.

That's a place, isn't it? Can you go there? Don't ask *me* how to get there. You should know how this works by now. You've done such a great job using your brain, so don't stop now.

If you want to get somewhere you need legs, right? Unless you want to walk on your brain and ears. Not happening. So, you *do* have legs. Can you see them? Whoa! There they are! Wait, why weren't they there just a minute ago? Because you didn't *need* them a minute ago. Now you do. It's really not that complicated. Nothing is worth seeing it if it wasn't first worth hearing, worth thinking, worth feeling. No shortcuts.

If you can see your legs, what else can you see? They have to walk on something to get to whatever is making that sound, right?

Oh.

There's the floor. You're standing on it. It's black but otherwise featureless. If there's a floor there has to be a ceiling, right? You look up. Well, not necessarily. There isn't one. What about walls? You don't see walls. The black floor just extends outward in all directions. Hold on though. If there's a floor, and it's "black," what color is all the other stuff? You know, the stuff to your left and your right and up above when you looked for the ceiling. You really don't know?

Huh. Okay. Well, you'll find out soon enough.

You start walking. The dripping sound isn't getting any softer or louder. You have no idea where it could be coming from. It would be nice if there were walls or *something* to show you how to get there. Alas. You don't know where it is or how to go about finding it. You only know where *you* are. And how would you know that?

Oh– that might help. There's a rope tied around your waist. Your waist? Where did that come from? Well, you can't tie the rope around your legs because you need those for walking. You can't tie it around your ears because that would hurt like hell, and you can't tie it around your brain because – well, then you'd be dead. And you're not dead. Remember? So that's why you need a waist.

The rope extends far into the distance, it's not resting on the ground, it's taut. Either that or there's no gravity here. But you're standing on the black floor, so there must be gravity. Okay so, the rope is tied to something. Let's find out. Shall we?

You take your first step and the rope gets slightly looser. The rope is linking you to something. What could it be? Is it the same thing that's making that dripping sound? You sure hope so. And then you *know* so because as you follow the rope, the sound gets louder. Not only louder but faster. There's less time between drops (if that's what they are) with each step you take. And you finally start to see some walls – one on your left and one on your right. You're still getting used to these eyes (if they're even eyes), but you are nearly positive the walls are getting closer and closer together, as if you're walking into the corner of a room.

The dripping sound grows faster still as you travel. The sound is bouncing around you. It almost feels like it's inside you, but not inside you. You can't really explain it. You're too busy looking at the walls. They're not (entirely) black like the floor. There are blotches of red, brown, purple, deep blue. Colors.

Colors. See? Told you you'd find out soon enough.

There doesn't seem to be any order to the color patterns but they're getting more vivid the further you go. They're also getting lighter. Well, not *getting* lighter, they *are* lighter. There's light behind them and it's illuminating the walls from behind. It seems they are at least partially translucent. Wait, now the floor is doing the same thing. And so is the ceiling that's now above you. You glance back in the direction whence you came. You see the old black floor and the "nothingness" around it and –

Oh, dear –

It's dreadful to look at. So cold and lonely. Utterly barren. Now that you've seen and heard and felt and thought, you don't want to go back there. No matter what.

You keep moving forward. The walls are closing in, but you're not afraid. This feels right. The sound is nearly upon you. You're super close. The drip has smoothed itself into a pour. You take a look at the rope and it's – it's slimy. It's not a rope. It's something else. You never really got a good look at it before, but here in the light, you can see more clearly. It seems to be made out of the same stuff that walls are made of.

You keep walking. You're almost there. You can see the corner of the room. The end of the road. And at the end of this road is a pool of water. You don't know why, but it's beautiful. You approach the pool. You look down. And what do you see?

You don't see yourself. At least you're pretty sure it's not you. You see two people: a man and a woman. There's no one else here, so who are they? Why are their images being reflected back to you and not your own?

Wait.

You don't know what you look like. So how would you know it's you anyway?

You speak, "Mommy? Daddy?"

Two booming voices reply in unison, "Turn around. Come to me."

You obey. The black floor is gone. So are all of the fleshy looking/feeling walls. It's all bright, white light and it engulfs you. It hurts. Get ready…!

…me? Oh. No, no. I stay here. I always stay here. Just like last time, and the hundreds of times before that. You go. It's great out there. I'll be here when you get back.

Okay. Don't be afraid. Ready?

There you are.

About the Author

Bestselling author of horror and dark fiction, Drew Starling is a husband and dog dad who loves strong female leads, martial arts, and long walks in the woods with canine companions. He would like to think his plots are better than his prose but strives to make his words sound both beautiful and terrifying at the same time. He listens to Beethoven, Megadeth, and Enya when he writes. His only rule of writing: the dog never dies.

Your Presence Remains

Sassa Brown

The wind whispers
Ever so slightly
Your name
Soothing my soul
My thoughts wander
To that distant, forbidden time and place
Where you were
And I
By your side
No one, nothing
Could separate us
Or so I thought

Circumstances arose
As they often do
Which stood between us
And alas I was forced
To say good-bye
Never to hold you
Never to tell you how I truly feel

My love for you never withers,
Never fades
The memories of our short time together
Are all that remain
Yet
That is enough

Enough to sustain me until we can be together again
And as the wind whispers your name once more
Embracing me
I stand here, taking it in
As though it were your arms around me

About the Author

Sassa is a publisher, designer, wife, and mother of two human children and three four-legged children. She has ghostwritten nonfiction books, articles, business manuals, and more. She also spent two years writing articles for online magazines. She loves to read anything she can get her hands on. Some of her favorite authors include Margaret Walker, Eudora Welty, H.G. Wells, Jules Verne, and Neil Gaiman.

****

From the Author

Your Presence Remains is dedicated to my grandmother who raised me throughout most of my childhood and was always there for me. She greatly influenced the person I became and was a guiding light for me, always pushing me and encouraging me to go after my dreams and to stand up for what I believe in.

Descent from Home

Julianna Rowe

What if no one was here? What if I don't come back?
Where is the reality?

It was an average evening at our home. Or was it still morning? I recalled lying in bed with my husband cradling his head in my arms like you would a child when I noticed what seemed like hundreds of sweating beads sitting stagnant on his forehead and more dangling from the black strands of hair above. He looked up at me and grinned in a suspicious manner. That unnatural smile told me he had a wanting of my flesh to satisfy his manhood.

Ordinarily, I would have joined in the pleasure of his company upon mine. But it was the sweat that pulled me away. I never liked a sweaty man near me. Guess that came from a bad experience I found myself in decades ago like many women have. I hadn't shared that with my husband and never would. There he was still staring at me like a wanting child ready to suckle the mother's breasts until the belly was full, always in expectation of the next feeding.

I simply could not be in a situation with sweat, so I gently slithered out from under the sheets and as I planted my feet firmly on the floor he said, "Okay later then." I turned and gave him that same unnatural smile affirming his statement would be brought to life later. But later never came.

The kitchen had been left a mess from the previous evening dinner. Steaks cooked to a fine pink to match the chosen wine along with fresh sautéed green beans. He was clearing the counters, and I was feeding the little dog and housecat. I noticed there was no water in their dish. I filled it and as I walked across the room to place it at its normal spot I commented to my husband in a rather harsh tone.

"What if I wasn't here? What if something happened to me, would you remember to give the dog and cat water?"

He stopped his kitchen chores, turned, and looked at me with uncertainty in his eyes and responded.

"What do you mean if you weren't here? Are you planning a trip or something else I should know about considering your tone?

I had set the water in its place and stood up red-faced from all or at least some of my blood rushing to my head. I had stayed bent down too long not wanting to rise back up into the situation I had created in the first place. I had no idea why I communicated to him in such a fearful, slightly harsh tone regarding what if something happened to me. As I stared at him rather blank-faced I felt a gray dread of some sort flash over me. A sensation I had never experienced before. It wasn't anxiety or was it? It came and went so fast if I had been busy, I might have missed it. They say that is how the spirit works. And then I came out of my self-induced trance, shook my head a bit, and responded in jest. Something I did when trying to cover up real emotions.

"Well, what if an alien ship lands and takes me away to another planet. Oh honey, I'm just jesting, can't you tell by now when I am joking?"

And so, we continued cleaning up our dinner mess from the previous evening, feeding the dog and cat, and various other household chores never mentioning my out of sort comments again. Our son visited that day with his two children. I spent an unusual amount of time on the floor playing with them. It was going into late afternoon when they left and we had not had dinner but were not very hungry considering all the cheese and crackers, ice cream, and cookies that had been passed around.

We decided to take the dog for a walk but noticed the sky an odd shade of gray. I asked my husband if rain or storms had been forecast. He replied that he hadn't heard but we both thought we should turn around and head back home just in case. The dog always liked it when we sat on the porch sometimes in silence simply enjoying life, its sounds, its smells, and its peace.

There was still a bit of an ashen look in the sky as night fell casting its shadow and hiding any hint of anything strange or out of place. The clock ticked on into the late evening when we realized we had not had dinner. My husband was already in his shorts and T when I suggested I make one of our twice-a-year visits to McDonald's for two Big Macs, fries, and chocolate shakes. He was willing to redress for the occasion and go with me, but I firmly said I could handle a quick run to Mickey Dee's on my own. It was getting chilly out, so I grabbed my jacket, keys, and phone and as I walked out, I went into my joke mode again.

I said, "Honey, don't forget to give the dog and cat water if I don't come back!" And then I laughed and shut the door behind me.

Shortly thereafter I received a text from my husband saying, "Don't be morbid, that isn't funny, stop it... I love you."

I sent him back three laughing with tears emojis. But I did wonder why I was joking about such a thing. How would I feel if he were doing that to me so, I let it leave my mind the same way it came in. However it came in, I had not yet contemplated.

I got to McDonald's before closing time which was eleven p.m. Our small town rolled up its streets around ten p.m. so I was out and about late for a weekday no less. I ordered the two Big Macs, fries, and shakes and asked where the lady's room was. The young man pointed, that way, which didn't really give me a good direction but I headed off anyway thinking it couldn't be too far. I pushed open a door I thought to be the restroom, and as it closed behind me, I realized there was no sign on the door saying what it was. I glanced around a large, dark room with many doors to other rooms. Maybe they were freezers or other such food storage areas. Nevertheless, I didn't like the feeling of the room, so I turned and reached to open the door expecting to leave immediately when to my total shock it was locked. I banged on the door and hollered but no one came. Why didn't they hear me? I turned on my phone flashlight and saw a wall plug on the opposite side of the room. Seriously, I didn't want to move; I was frozen by some unnatural, terrifying fear. I told myself to be calm because someone would come and find me eventually.

I always carried an extra phone charger in my purse for occasions just like this one, NOT! I plugged it into my phone and then into the wall but no lightning bolt showing a charge, nor did it show any signal bars at all. I still had the flashlight but no way of communicating with the outside world. I started checking those big, gray doors one at a time, each locked but also keeping in the front of my mind not to allow any of them to close behind me if, in fact, I actually got one open. I already felt like I had fallen into some crazy outer space rabbit hole. I was born with a vivid imagination that remained within me to this day.

And then it happened. The third door I tried opened to the outside world or at least I thought it was the outside world. I looked around and noticed that same chilling ashen gray we saw when we walked the dog earlier in the evening. But it was dark so, what was I seeing? The street was the normal street I drove on to get where I was, so I let the door shut. Was that my safe place I just closed myself off from? I walked around the building to the front, but everything was dark.

The employees must have thought I left without my food never even checking on me. Or maybe they checked the ladies' room, which I never did find, making this fiasco even more problematic. As I leaned on the glass door, I noticed a faint light inside and what I thought was a person moving around. And then behind me, the streetlights became brighter than they were before like "something" supernatural had given them an electric charge. I felt like I was in the worse crime area of the biggest city with crime lights surrounding me versus streetlights. And to the left of me a gang of boys out to do harm.

And then from out of nowhere, in a flash, the hugest round aircraft with a thousand lighted windows that reminded me of the million tiny fairy lights I had placed with diligence on our porch at home. Home! How would I get home and where was I?

I started to sob with fear at the glass window begging the worker inside McDonald's to help me, please help me but no one came out of the dimly lit darkness inside. Then I felt a hand on my shoulder, and I knew I was a dead woman. I screamed a bloody scream and said the words don't forget to give the dog and cat water.

My husband was shaking me near violently as I played out my rabbit hole disaster right there in our bed. It was me this time with beads of sweat dangling off my wet frightened strands of hair not to mention my brow. My husband didn't have a problem with sweat like I did thank goodness because I needed someone to hold me and bring me back from my outer space visit to McDonald's. I think I forgot to eat before we retired to bed that evening.

That was truly a terrible nightmare, yet it suggests how sometimes we really can't get back home for one reason or another. Whether home is our marriage, our life, our job, or a relationship. Occasionally, and I hope not too often, we need a strong dream to awaken us to reality and gratefulness.

About the Author

Julianna Rowe is truly a gifted writer of fiction because of her gift of imagination. She is a spiritual person, also. So, coupled with her imagination comes wisdom and insight into the enjoyment of other humans, the people who also possess the kind of fear that seems to excite the emotions, and yet they cling to a logical outcome to her stories. Those conclusions don't leave the readers cringing in fear. Instead, they leave the reader excited; yet satisfied.

Julianna is a prolific writer in many different literary genres. In all of her writing, her descriptive words transport the reader directly into the stories, making them part of the literary scenario which completely captures their interest until the end.

Looking Back
C.L. Williams

I've praised Heaven and I've raised Hell
No matter what I can still accept myself
I have been through the worst and I'm still alive
I've made some bad choices; I have nothing to hide
Looking back, I know I have been a disgrace
I can still look in the mirror with a smile on my face
Looking back, I've been a sinner and I've been a saint
It's my life and it is the picture that I paint
I accept the bad as it showed who I once was
I can now walk in the light and show my love
It doesn't matter because at the end of the day
I can accept the choices that I have made
Looking back, I see my mistakes and accept my growth
Because I've gone through things that only I know
I may have done bad, but I can now accept who I am
I can now get on my own two feet, I can now stand
You may not see it, but I've learned to accept myself
Because I've praised Heaven and I've raised Hell

About the Author

C.L. Williams is an international bestselling author living in central Virginia. He's written eight poetry books, four novellas, one novel, and a contributor to a multitude of anthologies. His most recent poetry book, *The Paradox Complex*, includes the poem "Sad Crying Clown" that was turned into a short film for MMH Productions YouTube Channel. Williams is currently releasing a series of novelettes under the banner *Chaos Fusion*. When not writing, he enjoys writing and sharing the works of other independent authors.

The Cord
C. Marry Hultman

Mr. Garfield is an ornery educator who most of all would like to be left alone. He is plagued by a slight birth defect causing him not to fulfill his dreams and viewing those around him with contempt. Although maybe being an educator can give him a purpose in life.

Click. Click...click came the sound of the bicycle lock as he first, inserted the key, then slid in the connector and then lastly turned the key again. He put his hands in the small of his back and arched back, *click...click...click* went his vertebrae as he stretched out. Pushing back his sunglasses on his nose, he turned to the sun already high in the sky, even though it was only seven-thirty in the morning.

It quickly became cooler once he closed the door. It was as if the air itself wafted across the marble floor, up the stairs, and then back down to the lobby chilled, very much like ice cubes cooling down pop on a hot summer's day. He leaned against the whitewashed walls for a moment to catch his breath. He could finally relax, out of sight from passersby.

Perspiration trickled from his head, along his neck and down his back like rivers feeding into one of the great lakes, and he could feel the fabric stick to his skin, melding, becoming one. While resting he considered climbing the ten steps to his office, exhausting his already tired legs or if he should use the elevator and risk the scorn of his colleagues.

The faux marble steps almost seemed to mock him. The design of contrail like stripes and painted on trilobites looking like smug, lurid faces against the gray. They were like all the other things in the building. An effort to try to appear hallowed, when in fact the institution was no more than eleven years old. Yet it tried to compete with the other giants of its kind in the area, and to do so it had to look the part, even if it became a mockup of an original. Just like him. A distorted reflection of a real man.

He stepped inside the small space and let the automatic door silently close behind him. Beep...beep...beep went the warning sound. Lights flickered on, one...two...three flashes, as he read the sign next to the buttons that informed riders that only eight people at a time were allowed to use the vehicle.

'Rules.' He thought to himself, 'everywhere these goddamned rules.' He traced the black, raised letters with one, sweaty index finger and then thoughtfully moved it to the button marked one. As soon as the elevator moved, he checked his reflection in the mirror. Apart from the perspiration covering, his body he felt quite pleased with his appearance this morning. Of course, that was how it always went.

He had often wondered if the combination of lighting and the type of reflective surface so common to elevators were specifically designed to make people look their absolute best, like the ones found in changing rooms at H&M. He only glanced at himself in a mirror three times in a day; getting ready in the morning, in the elevator, and in the evening, standing naked in his bathroom before stepping into the shower. Unlike this mirror, the one in his own home always gave a negative report, almost like the trials of the day had broken him down. It was as if the air left him completely.

He put the sunglasses back on and leaned against one of the walls. Once safely at his destination he used his key, then knocked three times on the wall, and then shouldered the door open, leaving a wet print on the glass. He looked at it with a smirk and the tiniest bit of pride at giving the custodian just a little more to do today.

He could just picture that round, face with its dark hue and hair dyed red cursing in her nasally voice. Heavily accented, as she had to spray cleaner and then wipe. Maybe there should have been more camaraderie between them; they had both battled their own form of adversary. She had pulled herself from the poverty of a third world country, continuously hollowed out by dictatorship and the modern-day imperialism that was Western tourism, by spreading her legs for one of the dirty white masters and allowing him to whisk her away to a better life in return for love… or was it lust?

He, on the other hand, clawed his way up from economic as well as cultural poverty by playing the game, adopting a persona and acting like those he understood to be above him, hiding his disadvantages and playing to his strengths, whatever those were. Meanwhile, he looked down on those he perceived as weaker, and, in this case, an overweight custodian from the Far East was definitely beneath him.

He looked around, only to find that the cafeteria, the first room one entered upon opening the door to the first floor, with its white office walls and red accent wall with the name of the brand in big bold letters on it, white round tables placed out in meticulous fashion, was empty. On the right side, off the cafeteria, lay the reception area. He peered around the corner to see if the receptionist Karen had arrived yet.

The ostentatious mahogany desk stood empty and unlit in the center of the room. He sighed with relief. He could still smell her perfume though and that meant she was around at least. Just as with the cleaner, he had no love for the trailer park dwelling middle-aged woman.

Sure, she tried to hide who she truly was with her bleach blond hair and tight curls, dressed in expensive clothing she more than likely had bought at Goodwill or at some *take an extra 75 percent off* sale at the mall. The scent she seemingly bathed in barely managed to mask the sour smell her clothes bore, evidence of someone who rushed their washing and put stuff away wet. For all her faults, the students seemed to appreciate her. Maybe it was because most of them were cut from the same cloth as her.

The fewer people he met in the morning, all sweaty and wheezy, the better. He detested showing weakness, his form already had him at a disadvantage, being tired from riding a bicycle was not a fact he needed spreading among the faculty as well. Moving across the abandoned cafeteria his limp, due to his gimpy leg was obvious. It was like the pattern of his life, a pattern one could design a dance around; 1-2-3, 1-2-3, 1-2-3. Everything in threes.

He unslung his backpack and placed on one of the black, rickety chairs close to the branded wall. He gave the letters a quick glance. He hated the connotation that the word brand brought with it. That a place of education might be reduced to a capitalist idea, making money off the youth of the nation. It was not the reason he had become an educator, to be honest, he was quite unsure why he had chosen that path in the first place. Most of his friends, former friends these days, would have laughed at him the day he decided to choose his major in college. Why would he want to go back to the horror that had been school? The wedgies, the scorn and ridicule, as well as the constant swirlies; one... two... three dunks in the toilet bowl. The treatment had not only conditioned him to duck whenever the boys passed him in the hallway, but also caused him to develop a stutter.

His mother had always told him *don't forget that the cord is no longer around your neck, don't let it continue to choke you,* and he tried to remember that, but all through school he could feel it tug at his throat and some days it almost killed him. Like it almost had on the day of his birth. At night, when he was lying alone in the dark, he could almost sense the rhythmic pressing on his little chest, one... two... three... 'live,' one... two... three... 'don't leave us.' The rhythm of his life.

He pulled out a clean flannel shirt, khakis, hard-soled shoes, and an overnight bag and walked to the bathroom that lay right outside his office, moving as quickly as he could to bumping into anyone. Because of his leg, it was not easy. The glossy laminate floor reflected the cold fluorescent lights overhead. A track that the cleaner had left. In the privacy of the cramped bathroom, not much bigger than the elevator, one could probably fit less than eight people inside. In there, the light was of a yellowish tint, giving those who tried to use the mirror a sickly appearance.

The teenage girls always kept the doors open in a vain attempt of letting natural light in. They were such fools.

As if, there would be anything natural in this place. It was fake to him. The thin white walls that could not keep the sounds of the corridor separate from the classrooms. The cheap laptops the students used, no more than stripped second-hand computers or the cafeteria lunches pretending to be nutritious. When they instead were chock-full of carcinogens and God knew what else.

He pulled off the damp athletic shirt and flung it against the wall with the tights soon following. He stretched out and gave himself a whore's bath with paper towels and soap, aptly provided by the company. Then he unzipped the overnight bag made from leather, pitch black with the familiar logo of Sergio Tacchini emblazoned on it. He never left home without it. One... two... three sprays. Meticulously, he removed a small tin of pomade, a steel-tooth comb, and a small vial of clear liquid.

With great care he scooped out the thick, beige cream and pulled through his still moist hair, he found that it being a little wet helped manage it, he didn't care it if was sweat or water at this point. There had been few things that he had been able to control in his life. The weakness of his right leg had made it difficult to become the athlete like the ones he idolized. His crippled hand had made him less popular than his obvious humor and social skills would have otherwise made him.

However, the hair, and later on his beard, was something he had complete control over, and he would manipulate and play with it until it was perfect, it had become a ritual at this point. He had let the facial hair grow long as was the style among the younger, fashionable set in the suburb he had settled in and he enjoyed the fact that strangers assumed he belonged to that group even though he had no interest in weird food or odd music, he was depressingly average. When his classmates would sit in the cafeteria and quote James Bond, Indiana Jones, or Star Wars, he could do nothing more than watch.

A couple of times, he would try to parrot the words his classmates used, but without the knowledge of the circumstances surrounding the quote his attempts would fall flat and he would be heaped with scorn. His mother struggled with money so cable, video rentals, comic books; the vehicles of cultural advancement were not readily available to him. His medical requirements had bled her dry, like the love his father was supposed to have felt. The man left before his son had turned two.

Once he had posted on Facebook; *Fate knows karate and it kicks me while I'm down. It spits me in the face as I beg for mercy.* No one had commented. People probably viewed it as pubescent, bordering on childish, but it was how he felt. His lot in life had left him bitter and thin-skinned when it came to adversity.

The sharp points of the comb gently scraped against his scalp causing the familiar sensation of pain against the skin, all part of the ritual, it kept him grounded, like a teenage girl cutting herself he had once told his therapist, who did not agree. He put the comb down, closed his eyes, pulled his fingers through the beard, and slowly opened his eyes. The image that met him was perfect, well as close to perfection he would ever be. After he got dressed and putting his tools away, he exited the bathroom. His shoes clicked against the hardwood floor in its uneven rhythm that told people who heard it that he was approaching. He always imagined that his colleagues stopped talking about him when they heard him coming.

The hallways and corridors of the building were like a labyrinth. There had never been any rhyme or reason for how they wound round the various classrooms and sometimes, weary visitors would find themselves coming to a pointless dead end. They would grab onto passing faculty with wild eyes as if the Minotaur himself might be waiting for them in the center of it all. It was understandable.

The corridors all looked the same. Sterile white walls with a red painted border only broken off by the occasional black scuff mark. No posters or artwork hung on them, for the principal found it tacky and messy. He wanted the school to be as faceless and bland as he was. This had caused the educators to turn their offices into reflections of themselves, bringing pictures of children, inspirational messages, or figurines into the mix.

For those who shared spaces with others, it had almost become a territorial war. Who could annex the room with the most personality? The first few weeks of working there, he had created his own Ariadne's yarn by memorizing every scrape and imperfection in the hallways. His ability to remember details had served him well in college but had left him devoid of a personality. He kept his head down and studied while the others partied and created contacts.

He felt the door to his office; he was the first one here, nice. Once he opened it, the familiar smell of a teacher's nook wafted towards him. He remembered it from the little room they forced him to occupy when he was in elementary school. Windowless with a single square table in the center, surrounded by beige bookshelves, stacked with large tomes. When his classmates were learning new things in mathematics or natural sciences, he was supposed to read aloud. It was to work on his stutter. An older woman, stout and with short gray hair, would sit with him and with an irritated voice try to encourage him. It was the smell of a student's frustration and a teacher's irritation and it had invaded his working space as well. In time his stutter dissipated, not vanishing completely, but the olfactory memory remained.

He shared his office with two others. Math teachers. He could not figure out why they had stuck him with math teachers. Due to his isolation early on, he had always found mathematics difficult. It had created a lifelong resentment towards that portion of schooling and one he had always wanted to see be reformed.

Once, at a weak moment, he had confided in a colleague that he wanted to start a podcast, one where teachers made fun of subjects other than their own. He enjoyed podcasts. There was something very simple and innocent about them and he believed that he would be quite good at it. He never ended up doing anything about it; after all, who would want to listen to him?

The room consisted of three walls covered by white bookshelves. Two large windows looking out over a park and three tables facing each other. Monitors and papers covered the desks. His especially. There were essays and tests everywhere, some stacked in piles several inches high. He sighed again. It was that time of year, the time when everything piled up. He pulled out his chair and sat down heavily.

'What's going on, homeo?' A voice cut through the brief silence.

He looked over to see a man leaning on the doorframe. He was dressed in black suit pants and shirt, a burgundy vest and sporting a red tie. Not really concerned with the rules of fashion. He was tall and wore his hair almost shaved, to hide his receding hairline, and had a neatly trimmed beard on his chin. Behind a pair of rounded glasses, he winked.

In many ways, Martin Holt was everything he was not. Sociable, well liked, and most importantly, carefree. He had been at the school since its inception and it had given him some influence with the principal. Where it felt like he chastised other teachers for the minutest thing, Holt came late, graded papers on his own time, and left early. All without repercussions. It was infuriating.

Meanwhile, he could not help but like the man, that was infuriating as well. He oozed charm and though he was married and had children, he freely flirted with the female staff without a care. Holt also came from an underprivileged family and compensated by dressing up his outward appearance.

Holt instead had fine motor skills and straight back. He tended to belittle those around him by making cultural references no one understood. When others quoted *The Simpsons* or *South Park*, he quoted *Baby Blues, The Critic, Dilbert,* or other forgotten cartoons. That and insulting them without them realizing he had done so.

'Nothing much.' He answered and tapped his index finger on the desk, three times. 'J-J-Just got in.'

'I see.' Holt had a Star Wars mug in his hand and sipped his coffee slowly. 'It's that time of year.' He indicated the paper.

'Sure is.' He did not even try to sound chipper; maybe his colleague would take a hint.

'You seem stressed.' Holt's demeanor changed. 'I mean, there seems to be something bothering you.'

'I'm just tired.' He said guardedly at this alien display of concern. 'Like you said, there is so much going on, I don't know where to begin.'

'Tell me about it. I just graded the essays of my English group. It just seems to get worse and worse every year. I don't think I've handed out as many Fs as I have this year.'

'I haven't started on the essays yet.' He said and rubbed his eyes with his twisted right hand.

'Well, then you're in for a treat.'

'Don't say that. I don't have time for that.' He could hear the annoyance in his voice.

'Well, good luck with that.' Holt said and gave a big smile. 'I've gotta go and check on Lindsey, she needed something.' He winked again and backed away. 'You've got a student waiting for you.' He yelled from the corridor.

Leaning back in his chair he contemplated the idea of talking to a student this early in the day. He would anyway have to recover the clothes he had left in the bathroom and reluctantly rose from his seat. He looked over his papers one time and tried to figure out the hours he would have to spend catching up on the grading. Found that it was too depressing to think about and left the office instead.

He bumped into a young man standing by the ill-placed Xerox machine right outside the bathroom. It was one of his students from English class; he changed his demeanor and smiled his toothiest smile.

'Raz.' He said and could almost hear the cheerful tone in his voice. 'What can I do for you at this early hour?'

'M-M-Mr G-G-Garfield.' It was painful to see the sixteen-year-old struggling. 'I-I wa-wa-wanted to catch you b-b-b-before anyone else ca-ca-caught you. I need help with the fi-fii-five pa-part essay.'

He nodded gently and put his hand on Raz's shoulder. 'Let us enter my o..o..office.' he said. 'I am free first pe...pe...period and can give you all my time.'

Raz sighed and they headed towards the office. Mr. Garfield left his things where he had flung them. It might annoy someone. Let them be annoyed; he did not care. Softly, he patted the boy on his back; one... two... three pats.

We all have cords around our necks; it is up to us if we let it keep choking us, he thought.

About the Author

C. Marry Hultman is a teacher, writer, and sometimes podcaster who is equal parts Swede and Wisconsinite. He lives with his wife and two daughters and runs W.A.R.G –The Guild podcast dedicated to interviewing authors about their creative process. In addition to that, he runs the website Wisconsin Noir – Cosmic Horror set in the Dairy State where he collects short fiction and general thoughts. Find out more about him at:
https://linktr.ee/C.MarryHultman

What Lies Within
Bob Byrne

Come and sit near the fire as I tell you a tale of What
Lies Within.

It's a story that has been told so many times that the truth has been shrouded in mystery, the details lost over time, but it's now time for the truth to be known. Listen well and know that here now is that truth. The beginning of the end started with a battle.

They had started as simple companions, adventurers seeking fame and fortune but had grown into friends and between two of them something more. They had fought back the darkness for years and now were finally toe-to-toe with the Dead King.

The throne room, the scene of this final battle. Magical energy plays a symphony broken by the discordant sounds of steel on steel. Sylo, the warrior, presses the attack leading the way as always with Khaz-gim the dwarven axe master guarding his side. A burst of energy flings them both back and the Dead King stalks forward a rictus smile forming around his dagger teeth. Darts of void energy streak towards these supine warriors slamming into a shield of pure light, dissipating harmlessly.

"Thank you, my lady," Sylo says as he jumps to his feet.

"My pleasure, oh brave warrior," Vadriel the Elven Mage smiles back, her easy tone masks the fierce concentration it takes to withstand the Dead Kings power. The Dead King recoils like a wounded snake from the light, giving Khaz and Sylo just enough time to recover and fight back. Sylo goes high as Khaz ducks low in an old waltz practiced on many dangerous dance floors.

The Dead King easily deflects Sylo's blade with his own, and the rictus grin returns; the Dead King begins to press his advantage, but he has fallen into a trap. He realizes too late as Khaz's axe alight with magic flame bites into his thigh forcing him to one knee. For the first time in the battle, the Dead King makes a sound, a scream that seems to emanate from inside his very soul.

Sylo sees his opening and takes it throwing caution to the wind in one last desperate bid to destroy this monster once and for all. Sylo's blade lovingly enchanted with Vadriel's own magical blood cuts through the Dead King's defenses. The tip of the sword piercing his rotten twisted heart. The Dead King falls back taking the sword from Sylo's grasp landing on a golden throne. With a last haunting gasp, he shudders and falls still. Only the Dead King's shell of a body remains, his hands wrapped around Sylo's gleaming blade in one last, futile attempt to pull it from his chest.

The party looks at each other in shocked silence. It is finally over; the years of hardship and pain are finished. Khaz speaks aloud what each of them is thinking. Those words that no one had really thought they would ever be able to say.

"What now?"

No one really has an answer for that. All their plans have been entirely based around finally defeating the Dead King. So much could happen that would likely change the story, perhaps for the better. They could grab any treasure they find and leave in search of a new adventure or simply flee. Instead, they decide to discuss what to do.

"The Empire is now without it's King. It's going to be chaos. We should get out there and try to help people." Sylo speaks up.

"Hmm, we could do that but there is another option," Khaz looks meaningfully at the throne as his beard fails to hide an impish smile.

"What do you mean? One of us takes the throne?" Sylo looks confused.

"Well, there is precedent. After all the Dead King wiped out all the potential descendants. If we do nothing then we are looking at Civil wars," Vadriel states.

Sylo never gets a chance to respond. The door flies open and the Dead Kings soldiers burst in. Upon seeing the corpse of their former leader, they turn their heads, as if one body, toward Sylo, who stands in front of the monster that haunted their dreams.

There are certain moments throughout history when the Fates stop weaving and hand the loom of fate to mortal men. Times when they create their own destiny. This is exactly one of those moments.

Sylo walks to the throne and tosses the corpse of the Dead King to the ground. The guards stand transfixed and then, as if blown down by some powerful wind, bend the knee and proclaim.

"Long live the King. Long live the King,"

Sylo sits on the golden throne and the world falls away. He sees himself dressed in gleaming armor a crown sitting atop his head. The words ALVEA TOL MESARA ring out. The vision ends as suddenly as it began. Sylo is back in the throne room.

Once more the friends come together to discuss events.

"Alvea tol mesara. Sounds like Ancient or even older," Vadriel says.

"What could be older than Ancient? I mean I heard they were the first people," Sylo asks.

"People yes but not the first beings. We Dwarves have legends of beings that populated the world before it was the world and their bones became the earth and rocks," Khaz explains.

"The Elves have similar stories, but they are mostly warnings. These beings jealous of the young races left artifacts, powerful beyond magic, to lead them to destruction," Vadriel says.

"Hmm, we have heard of those same artifacts, but we believe them to be left here to teach us," Khaz returns.

Sylo sighs aloud. If he doesn't intervene, they will argue for hours.

"Vadriel, try to translate the phrase I heard, maybe Khaz can help you. I feel fine and your spells detected no residual magic so it's probably not some kind of cursed item. In the meantime, we have a kingdom to rule,"

Three Years Later

Sylo proved to be a capable and just ruler for a time and the land prospered. But peace can never last, and as the land grew fat creatures filled with a dark hunger turned their eyes toward this prosperous land.

Sylo sits upon the golden throne listening to his Generals argue. Vadriel had long determined that the throne was not a cursed item and Sylo finds it comfortable. Each time he sits upon it he sees the same image and hears that same magic incantation. Sylo turns his attention from his throne back to his Generals.

"If we don't march, they will keep coming back. I say we march out and end it now," General Bracken beats the table as he speaks making sure that everyone is paying attention. He is a huge man who had fought back to back with King Sylo against the legions of the Dead King. He was a hard charger a harder fighter and prone to impulsive decisions but in the thick of combat with the panic, blood, and death, there was none better to have.

"I agree that a response is necessary but to summon the entire army might be unwise. These are small raiding bands of goblins, not an invasion force," General Hauser speaks so softly that it is difficult to hear him. He is a more cautious man who only speaks when he has considered his words. And his words are well-considered. Marching armies were a splendid sight but the devastation they left on the land could take years to recover from.

Sylo sits on the edge of his throne and looks at his third General.

"What do you say Khaz?"

Khaz leans back and strokes his beard.

"I think we need to march. We know where the raiding parties are camped. One swift blow and we could end them,"

Sylo nods as a solution is found.

"We march but we won't take the entire army. I think we can do it with a quarter. Here is my plan,"

Sylo takes a deep breath and laughs loudly. The chill of the morning air and the sounds of the forest truly waking him up better than any elixir can. His advisors had not been happy when he announced that he would be leading the army but if he had been forced to stay in the castle any longer, he might have gone mad. So much of his life was on the open road, and he misses it. He spends many long hours staring out of the throne room window wishing he was riding those paths again. This is not the same as his old travails though. Instead of just him, Khaz and Vadriel, fifty attendants wait on his every whim. He sleeps in a tall pavilion instead of the cold ground with a rock for a pillow. He has to admit to himself that he is enjoying these comforts if only a little.

His enjoyment of his freedom is broken by trumpets calling him.

Sylo rides to the front and sees Khaz waiting for him.

"We found them, just give the order and we can ride in," Khaz looks eager. Sylo understands the feeling, that anticipation mixed with fear that is the time before a battle.

"The word is given," Khaz smiles a feral grin, turns his horse, and rides away a battle cry sounding from his lips. Sylo moves to the hill to oversee the battle. A longing to charge into the combat pulls at him but Khaz had talked him out of it. From his vantage point, he sees things perfectly. The goblin camp was laid out in typical chaotic fashion with minimal defenses. The human infantry marches together in tight steel ranks only being kept from charging by screaming Captains on horseback. Arrows flyover their heads pouring death into the camp. Goblins attempt to rally but are cut down where they stand. It was never truly a battle but a slaughter. Those few raiders foolish or desperate enough to try to fight to stand are obliterated, their blood watering the ground.

Vadriel rides up next to Sylo.

"The goblin shamans have been dealt with," Vadriel says.

"Send the elves my appreciation," Sylo returns, a smile crossing his face.

Vadriel runs her hands through her hair and sighs. To her eyes, Sylo looks happier than he has in a long time. She knows that he feels the burden of leading the Empire every day. He comes to bed later and later and sleeps less and less. A messenger from the front rides up and hands a scroll to Sylo waiting for his response. Sylo opens the message and a dark cloud passes over his face.

"A report from our advanced scouts. They have found the goblins' main camps. It's filled with women and children and young fighters; it's mostly undefended. Bracken is asking for permission to attack and wipe it out," Sylo rolls the message up and sticks it in his saddlebags.

"Are you going to let him?" Vadriel asked fearing the answer.

"I don't know. The goblin young will grow up to be raiders as well. If we push the attack no child will have to lose his parents to a goblin sword ever again,"

Vadriel stares at the man she loves. In his mind, he has returned to a burning village listening to the screams of his family and friends. He is feeling the press of the broken dead hiding him from the goblins destroying his life.

"We aren't them," she whispers.

"What do you mean?"

"We aren't goblins. We are better than them. They kill innocent people; they haul us away as slaves. We can't become them," Vadriel hears the pleading in her voice and hopes her love will listen.

"You're right. We aren't animals like them. If we just ride away, they will be back next year and the year after that, and more people will die. ENOUGH," Sylo pulls out a scroll and quill and writes a quick message, and hands it to the messenger.

Vadriel opens her mouth to say something but Sylo is already riding away.

The ride back to the castle was much more subdued. Vadriel barely spoke to him and Khaz was conveniently absent. Sylo had ridden out to the goblin village after the battle and had seen the carnage. The image of tiny bodies being tossed on the funeral pyre ran through his head again and again. Maybe they were right, maybe he could have enforced some kind of peace, but the image of his own family's corpses pushed aside his guilt. They were monsters that needed to be exterminated.

He had ensured that his people would live in peace for generations. Vadriel and Khaz would understand that eventually. The news of the victory had spread, and they were greeted by enthusiastic people celebrating. Vadriel watched as Sylo smiled and waved to the people. She sees how easily he is being drawn into the role of a King, no longer the warrior she knew.

Sylo walks into the throne room and sits down. He prepares for the usual image of the warrior clad in silver armor and he sees what he expects, mostly. The eyes of the figure dart back and forth as if expecting a dagger from the shadows. Instead of hope, he sees fear.

A year passes and the kingdom grows again, but that growth brings new problems. King Sylo, for that is what he is, the adventuring warrior becoming more and more distant with each decision that he makes, sits again listening to the host of new problems.

"The western farmlands need water. We can build an aqueduct from Lave Ever," Chief Engineer Maren speaks up.

"The Elves won't like it. They consider those waters sacred," Khaz states.

"We could annex the land. It was ceded to the Elves after the Long War, but we still have a claim to it," General Braken suggests.

"The Elves have been good allies since the end of the war. They sheltered us during the fight against the forces of the Dead King," Khaz says.

"How badly do we need water?" King Sylo asks.

"We could be looking at famines. The war against the orcish hordes has drained much of the food stores we had put back," Maren informs the room.

"Then we have no choice. Take some soldiers and start building the aqueduct," Sylo orders.

The meeting brakes up leaving Khaz and Sylo alone.

"So, what happens if the Elves choose to fight back?" Khaz asks.

"Then we defend ourselves," Sylo answers.

"Is that how you'll have us justify it? Defense? We intrude on their lands and we call it defense?" Khaz grows angrier as he speaks.

"And what would you have me do? If we don't do this, we are looking at thousands of deaths," Sylo fires back.

"You didn't even consider the other options. When we were on the road-," Sylo cuts him off.

"We're not on the road, are we? All we had to do back then was watch out for ourselves and each other. Now I'm the King. Now I have to worry about so many people," Sylo shouts himself out and sits back down. Khaz notices the shock on Sylo's face as the magic of the throne does its work.

"Let me contact the Dwarves. We can dig some wells," Khaz offers.

"Okay. We will do that then," Sylo agrees and stands up to leave.

"I think it might be best if I replace that throne. It's uncomfortable," Sylo walks away.

Khaz watches him go wondering if he would ever see his friend again.

I would like to say that this is where it turned around, that the King listened to his friend, but this isn't that kind of story. The history books tell us how the decline of the kingdom began. About how the Orcs came back stronger and smashed King Sylo's armies. About how the treasury was depleted to hire mercenaries to push them back. Taxes were raised and raised again to pay for all of it and eventually the people could take no more. They rose in rebellion but were swiftly crushed. The headsman worked day and night putting the rebels to death and the crows fed well. What they don't tell is the effect it has on the King himself. How he skulked around the palace jumping at shadows screaming orders at phantoms. And the books don't tell how it all ended.

Sylo finds Vadriel in the throne room staring at the tapestries that had been used to cover the golden throne, a scroll clenched in her hand. She whirls around at the sound of his boots on the stone.

"Tell me it isn't true," Vadriel's voice is pleading mixed with anger.

"I have never been able to lie to you my love, but I had no choice," Sylo tries to explain.

"Is that your justification for everything? I had no choice. You sent your men to take the sacred waters of my people. You even didn't bother to ask,"

"And if I had they would have said no. The orcs poisoned most of the wells the Dwarves dug. The people need water,"

"Yes, the Dwarves who lent their assistance to help us. I saw the orders allowing your mercenaries to raid the Dwarven mines and the next round of executions. You aren't the man I love. You are a monster,"

Sylo charges, hands reaching for Vadriel's throat, but he has forgotten in his rage that she is no longer just a mage but an Archmage. Magic sears the air and Sylo is sent flying to the ground. He looks up to see Vadriel's eyes flash blue and another bolt of energy slam into his body throwing him into a wall. Sylo attempts to stand up but he is blown down again by a rush of magic and finds that he is unable to move. Vadriel walks over to the helpless King.

"I will let you live because of the love I had for you but if I ever see you again, I will destroy you. I am returning to the Elven lands now. Keep your soldiers out," Vadriel turns to go but remembers the scroll in her hand. She drops it on his paralyzed body.

"I translated the language of the throne. It means What Lies Within. It shows you your true self. What do you see now my former beloved? Are you still that warrior with the gleaming armor? I have not seen him in many years,"

She kisses his forehead for the last time, steps into a glowing portal, and is gone. Sylo's strength returns to his body and he stands up. He stares as the portal slowly closes. He has lost her.

She stayed with him through the years of fighting and pain, but he has driven her away with his actions. Sylo looks at the throne he has avoided for so very long and draws his sword. It is the same sword that Vadriel used her own blood to enchant, the same blade that had felled the Dead King so many many years ago. It glows again with an inner fire and he sees his face reflected back at him. It is a noble face, still fairly young looking seemingly just dipped in the stream of age. But is it his true face?

He walks over the golden throne pulling off the cloths used to hide it. He had tried to have it moved, but its magic had proved too strong. He sits now and once again the world falls away, once again he sees himself. Gone is that warrior in the gleaming armor with the compassionate face and the eyes of hope. Instead, he is face to face with the Dead King. The same rictus grin and dagger teeth, he knows without seeing that his once-proud heart is now shriveled and rotten.

He forces himself to look into its, no, *his* eyes and he sees the eyes of a broken hateful thing. He is transported back into the throne room and the image of the creature is replaced by his own reflected in the sword. For a minute he tries to convince himself that what he saw was a lie, but he knows better. This throne was a gift from those older than Ancients to rule wisely. The face looking at him from the sword is the lie. Sylo has seen the truth. He lifts the sword one more time. My friend has one more monster to slay.

About the Author

Bob Byrne wanted to be either a writer or a time-traveling archaeologist. He decided on writer when he found out that most of the time stream had neither air conditioning nor comfortable seating. The Gift is his first published book and he couldn't be happier.

For You I Wear This Mask
C. Marry Hultman

A short story told from two perspectives.
One of the narrators is faced with the annoying
woodworking teacher, Graeme, at an educator's
conference. He views the round figure with contempt.
The other perspective is that of Graeme,
who struggles with low self-esteem but is
determined to be accepted.

'Hello, my name is Graeme,' the portly young man said in a broad Scottish accent as he grabbed my hand. It was moist and uncomfortable. He held on just a little too long, and I imagined the kind of chafing one gets when wearing tight pants on a hot summer's day. He had forcefully pulled me closer when holding on, and when he released me, I felt that he was invading my personal space.

I estimated that he must be in his late twenties, but his pinkish skin, covered in minor blemishes and his failed attempt at a mustache made it very difficult to gauge his true age. He wore a dark blue suit that seemed to be two sizes too big, which was quite a feat for he was rather large, though most of the weight appeared to be centered about his waist and accentuated by the fanny pack – what we had referred to in high school as a bum bag – he wore.

I took a step back to become more comfortable and to get a better look at him. He grinned at me with a mouth that looked to have more teeth than most people sport. Some had crawled over the others, making it look like teenagers trying to pose for a picture, trying desperately to fit everyone into the frame.

'Man, it's hot in here.' Graeme said, perspiration already running down the side of his gigantic flushed face. It had flattened his hair, which he most likely must have done before he came. Now it was hard to tell, it was just a flat, a greasy mess against his scalp. He pulled out a handkerchief from the pack around his waist and patted his forehead as if he was afraid that he would smear some non-existent makeup. A tiny bead of sweat stuck to the end of his tiny upturned nose, and I could not help but focus on it.

'It seems as if we'll be working together at this thing.' He exclaimed with an exuberance that is usually only reserved to the very dumb, or annoying. Our respective jobs had sent us to the fair for some form of personal growth. I saw it as punishment for not playing by the rules, but Graeme, the jolly scot from Falkirk, as he would later inform me, seemed to be very excited to be here. If I was to hazard a guess, it was an excuse to get him away from the office for a few days.

'So, it seems as if you and I will be working and rooming together buddy,' he said as he crept in close to put his arm around my shoulder. He was uncomfortably warm. It was like standing next to a furnace and I tried to pull my shoulders together, to make myself small, and held my breath. 'This is going to be mental; we're going to have such a great time you and me.'

I nodded in agreement and secretly hoped that someone would come and save me from the situation. *Punishment indeed* I thought to myself. This was going to be the longest conference I had ever attended. These things were usually trite as it was; now, happenstance had added this Graeme character to rub salt into my wounds.

****

I had spent hours that morning getting ready. I had desperately tried to staunch the floods of sweat that just seemed to run from every pore in my body. I must have gone through three dress shirts just in one hour; the problem was that I had only brought the three. I ended up having to rinse through the first one and then use the blow dryer provided in the room to make it somewhat moisture-free. Once I had slipped the shirt over my head, the tie followed. My gran had tied it for me already at home on Weir Street in Falkirk, I could still, not for the life of me tie one myself. Looking at myself in the mirror, I found that I looked quite spiffy. I realized then that I had forgotten the deodorant, but I was not about to get undressed just to slap some of that on. Instead, I pulled the suit my father had lent me from its bag. He said it was a bit big, but after slipping it on I thought it felt very comfortable, better than the one I wore for my graduated, that thing chafed like a bitch.

The next step was the hair. For a conference this important, the headmaster would not have sent me here if he did not think it was important, I needed to look my absolute best. I had begun to sweat again, and I put one of the napkins from that little dispenser thing in the bathroom on my forehead to stop it from getting any worse. I must have put half the tin of pomade in my damn hair to try to get it into place, but it yielded the end.

I had quite a nice part going now; Barber MacDougall had nothing on this one, and I will be coming for your job next son. I grabbed my fanny pack and strapped it to my waist; made sure I had my money and threw in a couple of extra napkins to be on the safe side. I almost forgot to remove the one I had on my face.

In the lobby of the hotel, they had placed several papers on a corkboard. They were lists of names and next to the board was a table of bands with nametags attached. I found my name and slipped it over my head. On the board was the information about what group I was supposed to be in and whom I was supposed to share a room with. Nice. It was dull as hell staying in that room that the school had provided all alone.

The place looked a right mess, though, and I would have to pick up a bit before I headed to my new digs. Christ, I could already feel sweat roll down my neck and back. I was so looking forward to getting out of this monkey suit and back into my wife-beater and cargo shorts. I have always been so warm, sweat through everything, even in winter.

I must have looked a right ass walking from person to person, bent over in order to read their nametags. After what felt like an hour, I found him. He was a well-dressed figure who looked to have it all together. I took his hand and introduced myself to him. I hope I did not cause offense by my sweaty hands. He looks like a nice person, and I hope that we can get along.

People usually do not believe I have anything to offer by way of professional ideas, but the fact is that my students love me for who I am, and if they think I am a good educator, even if it might just be woodworking, then I am fine with it.

I think I rambled, but I crept close and put a sturdy arm around him to give him comfort. This conference would be the greatest yet.

Reflections of a British Bride
Shashi Kadapa

It is Colonial British India of the 1870s. Kate Middleton comes on a 'Fishing Fleet' to trap a husband. She is overwhelmed by the dog-like devotion of her taciturn husband Martin and the vivacious, tempestuous Andrew. Will she make the right choice?

Lisa Middleton Colby sat on her chair and gazed at the waving mango branches, laden with her favorite fruits. How stupid and lucky she was. Her husband was gruff, silent, but loved her. She was content. Her mind went back to the events of the past few months and she reflected on the happenings that had torn her apart and brought her back to sanity.

****

The first glimpse of India enchanted Lisa Middleton and her soul palpated as she looked at the scene from the deck of her ship. She gazed mesmerized at the flurry of activity on the dockyard and at the distant horizon where dark swamps and forests shimmered, creating a net of speckled emerald greenery.

India beckoned to her like a mysterious, veiled entity, which held unspoken promises and hopes.

The afternoon sun reflected from the sea, the glare blinding her. Brown natives in loincloths picked heavy loads from bullock carts, seagulls hovered in the sky seeking tidbits.

Oil stained waters lapped darkly against the ship, trying to push it back into the seas, as the tide rushed out. She peered from the deck in her salty and grime encrusted dress, sweat streaming from her brow, her heart beating fast.

'Was this hot, stifling, dusty place, to be her dream, her future, and home?'

The ship was one of the 'Fishing Fleets' that the British Government and the East India Company sponsored in the 1860s for unmarried girls, to find a husband in India. The company wanted its men to wed British girls, and not natives. Hence, it spent considerable efforts to bring unmarried girls from Britain to India.

The last of six daughters of a pastor in rural Hertfordshire, the lack of opportunities in meeting eligible bachelors in the parish, and her plain looks, meant that she was destined to remain a spinster.

Lisa was almost 20 and soon she would cross marriageable age, and this thought often made her get up in the night, gasping in terror. Often, she spent idle afternoons, watching summer clouds slowly evaporating in the summer breeze, smiling when they joined, feeling trepidation when they disintegrated.

A spinster in Victorian England meant a life of drudgery, having to wear hand-me-downs, and waiting for largesse from her married sisters. She liked books and music. However, these were not of much use in the marriage market.

Then someone had told her of India, where bachelor officers sought British wives. She applied to the Company, faced the interviews, and soon she was on the ship with a decent allowance that allowed her to buy trousseau and other necessities, and she was off to find a husband.

She endured many months of the cramped long voyage from London to Calcutta, fighting for her sanity, for privacy from the crew. The heavy seas made her retch and she often wondered if the voyage was worth the effort. Evenings, she looked forlornly at the horizon and her heart raced like a swallow seeking new winds.

During the long sweaty nights, she often followed the moon as it waxed and waned, happy when it shone full, depressed when it disappeared or hid behind clouds. She often felt helpless as the clouds that swam across the sky, shredded by the winds, taking new shapes, feeling lost and aimless, waiting for a shore.

As the ship approached the docks, she got down on her knees on the deck and prayed to the Lord, asking for help and guidance in this strange land. She prayed for a good husband and to be saved from the shame of being 'returned empty'. She was alone and feeling terribly homesick, and her legs trembled from fever and ague.

An officer greeted her, wrote her details in a register, and soon she was off in a rickety horse-drawn Tonga to her lodgings. The small lanes filled with the natives and the huge baskets that the native women balanced on their heads, amazed her.

Many of them had a loose cloth tied around their chest. They looked quaint, with their bottoms bobbing in the threadbare saree as they scampered on the roads, like the ducks on her farm. Thoughts of the farm made her desperately homesick as she came to terms with reality.

Her landlady was Mrs. Mathews, a kindly soul, widowed some years back, and who now offered boarding and lodging for young ladies from England. As she got down from the buggy and started pulling down her luggage, she was surprised when a swarm of natives rushed out to get her bags.

A long massage with warm coconut oil removed all the knots and aches from her body. A hot bath was kept ready and ayahs, the female native servants, gave a nice and long bath, washing away the salt and grime of her journey. Well, this was a welcome surprise for Lisa, since in England she could not even think of hiring a maid.

The ayahs addressed her as 'Memsahib', a respectful name for a White British Lady. They knew that she had come to seek a husband, and they hoped that Memsahib would take them along when she got married.

****

It took her a while to settle down in her lodgings. The warm sultry climate made her sweaty and drowsy, and she slept for the better part of the day. She loved to get up to the sound of birds twittering in the branches as they scolded and greeted each other. Daily baths were a must and her clothes were kept washed, ironed, and ready.

She would have continued to live like this until Mrs. Mathews reminded her gently of the purpose of her visit. She was a coal miner's daughter and had taken a liking to this shy and demure girl and wanted to help her.

'Get up and go lassie' she said. 'Good men are walking around, and they will be taken up unless you grab them first'.

Mrs. Mathews had clout in society, and she arranged for invites. So, Lisa started the rounds of the Calcutta Polo

Club, went to various balls, diffident, apprehensive, and bashful.

She was tongue-tied, not used to the snobbish fine people who put on airs, and flashed their husbands who had high positions, drove in fancy horse carriages, and wore scandalous dresses.

She felt like a plain hen among peacocks. Her demeanor was compunctious, she was blenching and tried to be unobtrusive, hiding behind people, not looking at the gallivanting men, who ignored her and thought her as supercilious and cold.

Gradually she got into the groove and gained confidence, smiled at men, and even accepted their invitation to dance. However, she always returned alone, without a man escorting her back.

Mrs. Mathews who chaperoned her on the rounds of husband-hunting was distressed at this exiguousness and her inefficacy.

It was almost two months since Lisa had landed and there was no prospective consort in sight! What a shame!

'There is a deep bias and provincialism here lassie. You have to be someone to get a good man. The spinster dowagers, who were born virgins and will die as virgins are the worst. They watch from the sidelines, drinking free sherry and gin, and act as matchmakers. I never could get along with them.'

'Let us have a look at your wardrobe'.

'My, my girl, these dresses will get you an old widower', she cried at the prim Victorian dresses with laces, frills, flounces, lace, braid, fringe, that confined rather than liberated her. The strings and ties wound up to her neck, hiding her form and shape. She called over a seamstress who spent a quick afternoon altering the dresses.

The result was a figure-hugging ensemble that scandalously exposed the top of her ample, milky white breasts. Lisa was a big girl, used to a hard rural life, and her figure was taut. The altered dresses now fell decorously around her waist, hugging her thighs and waist. Thinking of her mother and sisters, she argued in vain that she would never, ever wear the dresses.

Her chaperone said, 'Sure lassie, they would not allow it. But they are not here. So why bother, play the game as the cards fall.'

At her insistence, she donned the dress and stepped out, feeling very self-conscious. She felt as if the whole world was looking at her. She thought she looked like one of the bulls that the natives decked up garishly for festivals.

She looked good in the dresses. Her straight walk, the bouncing breasts and tight bottom, and her flushed, clear skin drew envious glances from other husband hunters. Wonder of wonders on the very first outing, a smart, strapping gentleman stepped out to take her hand as she got down from her buggy at the monthly ball, held at the Calcutta Presidency Club.

His name was Martin Colby, apprenticed with a trading house, due for promotion and posting as a district in charge. A large big striding man with arms the size of a young oak tree, a face rough-hewn and burnt brown with constant exposure to the sun, with untamed striking looks, a girl would have swooned in his arms.

'Get him, girl,' urged Mrs. Mathews.

'He is a good catch. I know him. His father was a Colonel who died some time back in the mutiny. He lost his mother when he was just seven. It does not matter.'

'Many girls have tried to get his attention. None succeeded. You get him, we will tame him,' whispered Mrs. Mathews.

A brief period of courting began that left her emphysematous. Martin was gentle but brusque, and taciturn. The long rides in his buggy when she sat on the front seat with him as he drove were exhilarating.

As the buggy swayed in the potholes and jerked to the sides, she managed to brush against his broad shoulders. Sometimes, when the road got rough, their legs touched briefly, sending warm shocks to her core, and she shamefully realized that she wanted him.

She longed to speak, chat, pour her heart out, hear his story, but nothing of that sort happened. She talked of books and music and even coaxed him to attend a few musicals. She felt aghast and shocked when she found him snoring through the program.

The lack of dialogue often left her wondering if he really cared for her. All he did was to glance at her with his big liquid eyes.

'It is like taking a dog out for a walk, or even worse, sitting with a log' she remarked to Mrs. Mathews.

Lisa was talkative with people she liked. She told him her life story, about her sisters, the life at her home, the dogs, her school, and about anything that came to her mind. Martin just gazed at her, not uttering a word.

He first held her hands for almost two minutes, as they strolled along the Hooghly River bank. The warm touch of his calloused hands melted her. She longed to be taken into his arms and she wanted to give herself up to his warm embrace, just like the heroines in the small books that she and her sisters smuggled in their petticoats.

'Take care Lassie', hissed Mrs. Mathews as she followed them. 'Keep your legs crossed tight. There are some things that hold a man and get him to marry and some that don't.'

She continued, 'Draw him closer and let him propose, then you can let him kiss you'.

Propose he did, one fine night when the fragrance of the Chameli flowers filled the garden. He stuttered, stammered, like a wet shameful and guilty puppy went pitifully down on his knee and proposed in a broken voice.

'Lisa', he gasped, fighting for breath and almost gagging. Clearly, the effort was more than what he could manage, "Will you marry me?" he gasped.

'Yes', she uttered. One simple question, one brief answer, and her life now joined his life.

She wanted to fling herself in his arms but managed to control herself. There was no thinking of what she would have let Martin do if he wanted.

Mrs. Mathews played a spoilsport and butted in, coughing loudly and breaking the charmed silence.

After congratulating the couple, she set about doing practical things like preparing for the marriage. Martin did not have any relatives, just a bunch of friends, who trooped in by the dozens.

Writing to Lisa's father and asking him to travel to India for the marriage would have taken a year, and this delay would not do. Lisa sent a letter instead, telling them about her life, her fiancé, and how good he was.

Mrs. Mathews arranged for a father for the bride and groom, and the marriage was quickly arranged in the St Andrews church. Lisa cried copiously in the arms of Mrs. Mathews, who had fortified herself with a full bottle of the finest Highland Whiskey, and she cried out her eyes too.

As a parting gift, she let Lisa take her favorite ayah, Laxmi, a middle-aged native, who had run away from her abusive husband and had sought refuge with Mrs. Mathews. She had promised to treat the young Memsahib as her own daughter and advise her on the best course of action.

****

Lisa waited in trepidation on her first night, waiting for the consummation of her marriage. She had read countless books and had dreamed about the nuptials.

She expected to be taken into her husband's arms and imagined they would spend a long time whispering sweet nothings to each other while she got ready mentally, and then she would give up to the passion.

Well, the reality was different.

She waited and waited alone in her room, while Martin and his friends drank themselves to hibernation. When she was almost asleep, she heard him trudging up the stairs, and then he entered the room.

Through half-closed eyes, she could see him standing by the side as he kept gazing at her. Then he unbuttoned himself and began groping. It felt horrid, for what seemed like an eternity, and then it was over. He rolled over and went to sleep.

She looked at the snoring form with disgust. She felt discombobulated, used, and humiliated.

'Where were the romance, the sweet whispers, susurrations, and gentle kisses? Were these just imaginations that some frigid author had concocted? Was this marriage?'

She realized that this man did not love her. He did not care for her, and she was just an asset, something to show off to his friends.

All her dreams of having a companion with whom she could converse intelligently were gone. She cried herself to sleep, ruing her misery and the cruel trick that fate had played on her. Her dreams melted away like a ball of butter placed near a fire, congealing into a mess.

The first few days after her marriage were very hectic. She played hostess to a number of ladies who dropped in to see her. Nights were spent visiting various balls and events, where she glided on her husband's arm.

Lisa had realized that this boor did not like books, the theatre, music, but the only things that mattered were hunting, horses, guns, tobacco, and other stuff that she loathed.

Within a week, her husband announced that he was promoted and was in charge of a trading post in far off Puna, off the west coast of India. The grief of parting from Calcutta that she had come to like was sharp. She liked the city, its fish markets, and the newly laid out streets that thronged with life.

She cried since she had to part from Mrs. Mathews, who would drop by often to her house. However, the shifting was not to be avoided, and soon she was busy getting her household goods packed and they went by steamboat to Bombay, a port town, and then onwards to Puna by land.

****

Their colonial house in Puna was grand and the pleasant weather was just great, different from the hot and humid weather of Calcutta. The rooms were large and airy, the gardens and lawns carefully tended by gardeners, the garden was filled with fine smelling flowers. Butterflies and bees flitted about, while birds chirped in the trees.

She settled down in her house and began the series of visits to other ladies, inviting them over, and spending quiet afternoons in the Gymkhana club playing bridge and Gin Rummy.

As she sat in her rocking chair, she pondered on her husband, marriage, love, and life. She realized they must have spoken just a few sentences all these months.

Other than looking at her in silence during the evenings when he was at home, they hardly exchanged any words. She was not interested in the trading and politics of the town, and they had nothing in common.

Worst of all, she was not getting pregnant, and this tormented her but not him. It did not matter to him if they did not have children. She had a faint feeling that he just wanted her to be around the house.

However, his brusque and silent nature was getting on her nerves. She felt stifled, wanting to break out, yell, shout, laugh, live life, and that was not happening.

That he cared for her beyond his life was clear. Once she was taking a bath in the big bathroom when she heard a hiss. Ignoring it, she continued pouring hot water on her body when he happened to glance up and saw a dreaded Cobra, with its hood raised. It was flicking its forked tongue across and stared at her, ready to strike.

Lisa shouted at the top of her voice, and in an instant, Martin broke the door and was inside. He threw a blanket over her naked body and gripped the snake by its tail, twirled it around, and dashed it against the wall, killing it.

He gathered her in her arm, his face close to her ears, whispering that it was all right and he carried her to the bedroom, depositing her in the care of the Ayahs. What thrilled her was not the snake, but the fact that her husband had come running in, like a knight in shining armor, just like in her books.

****

By an unspoken law, White women were not allowed to mix with native men or speak with them unless they had some work. With her husband busy, Lisa only had Laxmi, and other white ladies for company.

These ladies bored her since they wanted to talk only about dresses, trips, and scandalous stories of how their friends slept with other white officers.

In the meantime, she had come across a Piano and was trying to learn the instrument. This learning took away her frustration, and she spent time vigorously, hammering away at the keys. There was no one who could teach her since the few people who played had left for postings in other locations.

That was when she was introduced to Andrew Smith, a young scholar from the UK who had come to India to make his fortune

****

Andrew was the opposite of Martin. He was talkative, sharp, well-read, loved music, and even offered to teach her the piano. The other ladies were aghast at this development and started gossiping.

One of them was an old crone, Mrs. Snider, a dowager, bent and rheumy, whose main vocation was to visit all homes, gather gossip or make it up when there was none, and spread it around.

That is how the ladies came to know that old Mr. Timberlane was having it off with his maidservant. Mrs. Snider had sworn that she had peeped through the hedges and seen him enter the tool shed with her and then he had come out hot and sweaty, hurriedly buttoning his pants.

She was also the first person to spread the scandal of Mr. Cooke, the Parish priest, and an apprentice nun whom she had claimed to see 'in the stress of undress as he thrust mightily and heavily into her spread legs'.

Her audience never took her words seriously since she was known to make up the stories to get an afternoon of free Sherry and gin that she drank copiously like a dockyard worker.

However, this story of Lisa and Andrew seemed true. They had seen her looking attentively at him as he acted out bits of Hamlet and Macbeth and had laughed heartily as he acted various parts of The Comedy of Errors.

However, what got them the most was the manner in which she curled up before the piano as he flashed out a few Bach scores.

It was as if she was mesmerized and deeply infatuated with Andrew. Early afternoons she would come to the Puna Gymkhana and wait for her beau to come. Then the two would wander around the grounds, speaking of books, drama, and theatre.

They were made for each other, youth calling to youth, however, Lisa was married to another man, and this would end in tragedy, predicted a senior member of the gossipers.

Lisa skillfully introduced the subject of her piano lessons to her husband one evening when the mosquitoes were buzzing furiously, trying to get to the naked couple.

She was felt cold and empty as he thrust himself into her, groaned, and rolled off.

Knowing that he was satiated, she spoke of a piano teacher. "Martin, do you mind if I take lessons from him."

'Eh what?' he grunted. 'Piano lessons? Well if it makes you happy, then go ahead', he said before snoring off to sleep.

The lessons allowed her to meet Andrew in the privacy of his house and soon he was instructing her in the fine art of caressing the keys to get them to play a fine melody. Since she was a beginner, he held her hands and fingers and glided them on the keys.

The warm touch, the caressing fingers, his hot breath as he breathed down her neck, sent tremors inside her soul. This is how she had dreamt her life should have been.

They spent long afternoons in seclusion, and she trusted him as he played with her fingers and held her elbows to guide them, nuzzling her shoulders. Then he tried to kiss her, all the while whispering that he loved her, and he started pulling at her laces and cupping her breasts.

This was too much for her, and the years of prim and upright bringing shook her up. Her mother's warning that men wanted only one thing came rushing out from her memories.

Lisa jumped back from the chair and stood facing him. "No Andrew! This is too much. I like you but I cannot be yours, at least not right now" she gasped.

A repentant Andrew went down on his knees and spoke imploringly.

"My beloved! I am sorry, but you have consumed my soul and I could not live without you. I beg you to forgive me. I will wait until you are ready."

She rushed out to her home and saw her husband was sitting on the veranda, smoking his pipe and cleaning his shotgun as he gazed at her silently.

"Something wrong dear", he growled. "You came in a tearing hurry. Your Piano class is over?"

Muttering that she was not feeling well, she rushed into her bedroom and lay down. The encounter with Andrew had left her stunned.

She longed to be his, to enjoy fine arts, music, and books. She felt like a new person when he was around, and she felt confident, happy, and she laughed.

In contrast, her home was drab, without any sound, dull, stifling, despondent, and confining. She realized that there was no love here, only obligation. In any case, her duty to her husband and his reputation mattered most. If she ran away, then his name would be dirt. So, she stopped visiting the club and stopped seeing Andrew

****

By March end, searing summer winds started sweeping across the plains. Puna was not spared, and Lisa sat in the restive, airless heat as the servants waved the Punkah, huge handheld fans.

The languid heat made her sweat inside her bulky clothes that she was forced to wear. She was a British woman and had to be modestly clad at all times since natives were always around. She was forbidden to even expose her ankles in the fear that it would arouse a native.

As was the custom, the men and their families set off for Matheran and Lonavala, small hill stations nearby. These places offered some respite since the hills, the thick forest, and a cool breeze drove away the prickly heat.

Martin, Lisa, and Laxmi set off to Lonavala, where they would spend the summer in a beautiful cottage with a large garden and driveway.

Small groups of ladies and their children had settled down at the clubhouse, and Lisa hurriedly washed herself to go to the clubhouse where a gin and tonic awaited her. The sound of piano and singing wafted through the open windows. Her heart jumped when she saw the familiar profile of Andrew as he played a racy ballad.

Quietly, she stood in a corner not looking at him, yet casually glancing at him from the corner of her eyes. Andrew did not appear to be aware of her presence until one of her friends from Bombay dragged her and introduced her to him.

"See Andrew, this is Lisa, she is from Puna and plays the Piano".

They stared at each other, and she felt her legs growing rubbery. The long walks, the hours of talks, and the afternoon came back in a rush. With a start, she realized that she still cared for him. They spent the afternoon with others, and it was in the evening that Andrew managed to get her alone.

"Well, darling, nice to see you here. I still smart from your last rejection."

"Well, it's a thing of the past Andrews", she gasped. "We can start again."

In her desperation at getting him back, she was ready to be his. The ways of a woman are strange. If a man goes after them, they feel high and mighty and put on airs. If they are spurned, then they run after him.

Andrew toyed with her passions, speaking with her on some occasions, ignoring her in front of people, and then taking off with some other girls who had arrived from London. Full acquiescence was what he wanted from her.

He wanted her soul, her passion, love, and her body. He broached the subject again one day when they were sitting on the veranda of the clubhouse that overlooked the deep ravines and jutting hills.

It was summer and the plains were a roiling mass of heat waves that rushed up and dissipated on the mountain slopes. Light clouds were beginning to form, signaling the start of the monsoons.

In a few weeks, rains would drench the parched land, transforming them into lush fields and blossom with plants and grass.

The land would burst forth with life, fee from the fiery embrace of the summer. Koels would start singing, as would countless other birds and the chirping of insects would resound in the night.

Fireflies would set up a carpet of flickering light that mesmerized Lisa, and she longed to burst out of the caged life that her marriage had become. She dreamt of joining her, unshackled from the loveless torment of Martin.

Andrew dropped a bombshell.

"Lisa, I have a new posting in far off Meerut. I have to leave in ten days. Do you want to come and spend the rest of your life with me?"

He implied that there were other girls available, and he was doing a favor by inviting her.

The love blinded Lisa immediately wanted to say yes. However, she could not leave without telling her husband. She had a vague notion that he knew of her dalliance with Andrew, but he had never asked about the long hours she spent outside. It appeared to her that he did not care.

Her biggest problem was about telling him that she wanted a divorce and go away. He was a very strong and big man, and she was afraid that he would beat Andrew to death. The ten days seemed to fly and on the last day, early in the morning, when he was sipping a cup of tea, she decided to stoically bite the bullet and speak out to him.

Steeling herself, she sat across the table and said, "Martin, I want to talk to you."

Raised eyebrows were the only sign that he had heard and was willing to listen to him.

"Martin, I am going away. I have decided to go away with Andrew."

No answer, just stoic silence. She expected that he would shout, rant, protest vociferously, and beg her to remain.

In a boiling rage, she cried, "don't you care? You never loved me did you, Martin? I was just something you wanted for the physical release. You never bothered about what I liked, what interested me. My god! Why did I put up with you all these months?"

Laxmi came in just then and said, "Memsahib, Andrew Sahib has come with the buggy and he is asking you to hurry up."

"Go and tell him that I will be out in a minute."

Turning back, she shouted, "You do not want to even answer me?"

No response and she got even angrier.

"It takes two to make a marriage successful. We never talk, laugh, or even fight. This house is a brig."

At last, he said, "Go, Lisa, if it makes you happy, and if that is what you want."

She turned back for a last scornful look and paused as she saw the giant frame shaking with heart-wrenching sobs, tears running down in rivulets down his craggy face.

She was aghast!

Her husband, this hulking brute could cry!

He had so much pent up emotions, she never knew he could feel sorrow or joy, and she could never imagine that he could cry!

Unsure, she came back and stood in front of him, and hands reached out to caress his head.

All the womanly instincts came out as she held his face. In the months of their marriage, she had never caressed his face or run her hand through his hair, or even kissed him. Martin buried his face in her skirts and started crying out in loud sobs as he talked about his childhood.

"Lisa dear, my strict army father hated any show of sentiments, love, and affection, and I was caned if he cried or laughed."

He continued, "I vividly remember dear" he sobbed. 'I was seven when my mother died. I was made to stand at attention beside the coffin for hours and look straight ahead, just like the soldiers."

Wiping his tears, he mumbled, "I was not allowed to cry, even though I wanted to run to her coffin and embrace her one last time."

Sobs wracked his body and he cried, "There was no love, or emotion in my life, only discipline. It was discipline in the strict school where shouting and laughing was not considered gentlemanly, and discipline in the army camps where I grew. It was caning, punishments until I become one mass of unfeeling stone."

He choked up, his cries drowning in his throat. She held him tight against her stomach, her fingers clenching his hair.

"When you said yes", he sobbed, "It was the most wonderful thing that ever happened. I was changed, transformed, all the hardness had melted away, and I had something to live for. I wanted to take you in my arms, hug you and tell you how much I loved you. But my upbringing held me back."

He was quiet for an instant then began, 'Showing any feelings of love meant I was weak, that was my upbringing. In Calcutta, when you kept talking about your family, I was wonderstruck at the good memories you had. My only memories are of punishments and hard discipline."

He kept silent for a couple of breaths and began crying, the sound muffled by the skirts as she held him close.

"I would spend the night, just staring at you sleeping in the soft moonlight. You are everything to me, I just wanted you to be around. I vowed never to hurt you. I am ready to die for you."

Lisa stood with her mouth open. He regained his breath and then began in ragged gasps.

"Yes, I knew about you and that fellow. However, I kept quiet and consoled myself that were happy and found what you wanted."

"I died a thousand times dear, in bits and pieces every minute, knowing that your heart was given away. You were not mine, and I had no right to keep you. Hence, I kept quiet, my love', he wailed."

He sobbed, 'Don't leave me, dear. I will be an empty wreck, an abandoned ship."

He cried one last time before he buried his face in her stomach, his sobs shaking his large body.

Only one thought flashed through Lisa's mind as she held his head tightly against her stomach.

'*She was throwing away this! For a piano player! What a fool she was!*'

Laxmi came running in.

"Memsahib, Andrew Sahib has started leaving and is waiting at the gate and wants you to join him immediately. He is getting angry, what shall I tell him?"

"Please tell Andrew to go away. Please tell him that I am staying with my husband who needs me. Tell him never to come back here again."

"I will do that Memsahib", grinned the tearful Laxmi and added, "Memsahib, you have done the right thing."

Lisa turned back to her husband, and they walked to the bedroom to begin a new life. It started raining just then, the rains washing away the dirt and heat, giving new life, new hope, and the clapping thunder drowned out her cries of pleasure.

****

Lisa got up from her chair to greet her three children who rushed in shouting and laughing. Her husband Martin waved at her as he asked the servants to unload the provisions he had brought. The reflection was broken, but the spell lingered.

About the Author

Based in Pune, India, Shashi Kadapa is the managing editor of ActiveMuse, a journal of literature. His short stories have appeared or shortly due in print anthologies of Casagrande Press, Anthroposphere (Oxford Climate Review), Alien Dimensions #11, Agorist Writers, Escaped Ink, War Monkey, Carpathia Publishing, Verses of Silence, and in online publications of Spadina Literary Review, Nymphs Publications, Schlock Webzine, and others. He has written for The Times of India and Debonair.

The Murder of Eden Barker
Julianna Rowe

A soul caught in a dream state can reveal the truth. From the lies held in death bring forth the ghosts of responsibility.

Chapter One
The Vision

Mickie

Sitting, lying, or even standing on any beach has never been one of my favorite places to be, as it is most peoples. But this day was different in many ways. I had just finished several years of what else can go wrong. That was when one of Harris's friends offered me the use of his home that happened to be very close to the ocean. Very close. And it was free.

I took him up on his offer, which seemed far better than checking into the 6th-floor psych ward. So, I found myself walking in the sand washed with the ocean's brilliant blue-green waters daily. It was like I had joined a refresher course in getting born again. All my sins were taken. The earth was cleansing me and my soul from the bottom up.

Never had I experienced such a transformation of earth to spirit. It was as though I were passing through to another dimension. Each granule of sand manifested itself alive giving me a path to see beyond the limitations of this plane. Not only to see but to hear such a peaceful yet frightening moment in time. I didn't ask if I would be able to return to the "old" me or if this was a new world where I would remain. I simply drank in the existence of something clean and refreshing moving through every cell in my body while I continued to walk on the hot forgiving sands.

When I awoke, I found myself near an area of dried reeds. I had no conception of time at that moment. The sun setting still left a warm breeze that allowed me the comfort of staying longer. It was then I recalled the boy talking to me. I sat up and looked around, but I saw nothing at first. Words and pictures were penetrating my brain like a train at high speed.

Suddenly, it all slowed down... way down to a graveling voice likened a 33-rpm vinyl record. I had not yet learned to control or even sense properly the gift I had just received. All I knew at that moment was there was the body of a young woman lying two feet from me in the reeds and a young man leaning over her.

He tried to kiss her lips. And strangely, I could feel it. But they were dead lips. He didn't understand why she would not move. He tried to open her mouth with his lips as though they were still making love in the real world, but she had no response.

The young man appeared to be from another time. Knickers and a vest over a blousy white shirt. A cap that resembled one of those denim striped caps like the train engineers wear only this one was brown. An English looking chap I believe as I look back upon it.

I never saw physical emotion from him during his visit. Yet I saw and felt his spirit yearning for the girl's love through her lips. And then he moved over near me. He was on his hands and knees looking at me from my right side and back about two feet as though he couldn't get any closer. Like there was a veil between us. I wondered why he could touch the young woman but not enter my space.

I was not afraid. It felt more like a waiting period, where time and space had to come together in some sort of equation, I was not familiar with. Such as from physics. Me, I had the creative genes, not the $xf=xi+ \frac{1}{2}(vxi+vxf)+=y$, which stands for a "Position as a function of velocity and time. Even though I didn't know physics, I knew that was what was happening. Oddly, my mind also knew it without having so much as forethought of it.

And then he spoke to me. He told me his young maiden had been murdered. She was unable to move onto the after dimension he resided in. He was to be moved to a new dimension, but he refused until she could join him. He was in a grey holding pattern until she could release herself from the evil that took her life. She was also in a dark holding pattern and he calmly begged for my help. No other human had ever been able to hear him before that day.

I had been granted a gift from the Universe to find this young girl's murderer and set her free to reunite with the love of her life. The young man that had made her a woman lies in waiting unable to communicate or feel the touch of his lips upon hers, neither in the spirit nor in flesh. Yet I could feel both of them.

I looked toward the sky trying to find my bearings. I felt as though I had been in a tunnel of love but with disturbing dreams of murder.

Wow that was an amazing yet DISTURBING dream I thought. I was walking back to the beach house when the realization came to me that possibly it was not a dream. *Could that be?* I thought.

I didn't sleep well that night. The next day, I traveled to the local library and researched unsolved murders in Enaid City. Her body was found on the North Shore Beach near a group of reeds in the early hours of May 5th, 1893. Her name was Eden Barker. She and her friend, Johan Cline, had been brutally murdered while sleeping on the North Shore Beach. No weapon was found nor were there any clues. The couple had recently arrived in America from the United Kingdom. Eden had found a nursing job at the local hospital, but Johan had not yet secured work.

Dear God, what had I stumbled upon? I began to try to wrap my head around the how and why, not to mention the far away voices I kept hearing in my head at various times of the day. I recall beginning to wonder if I was losing my way in terms of my mind.

Chapter Two
Vacation

After spending a week of my vacation time searching the local library for any information on the Murder of Eden Barker, I decided to take get away from it for a while. I had not had time away from raising children or work for over three decades. That said, this was more than a vacation for me. It was heaven away from earthwork. Yet here I was on a strange beach given something wild and crazy from the heavens, I thought anyway. But then maybe I was given this from HELL to ruin my only time away from responsibility in years. How would I know?

We had been married for less than a year. Harris and I were High School sweethearts long past. We rekindled our love later in life. We had a kind of puppy love that turned out quite real. We just couldn't seem to be apart even though we struggled to be together. In the past, neither of us could understand the why of our deep connection. Then he married another as I did also. We both had children from the previous marriages, and it wasn't until years later we rekindled our love.

I recall every time I would look at a certain photo of him from the war I would cry. A photo I never saw until we had rekindled our love as he went to war during the period we were apart. I didn't know why I would cry except that I missed him terribly. Missed him how? Why? We always joked a bit that maybe we knew one another in a previous life.

Harris was a tender man with a harsh voice at times. He was the love of my life and I his. Even though we certainly didn't agree on much. There were many times neither of us could figure out why we were together. Yet we couldn't find a way not to be. We tried to separate many times, only to be drawn back together again and again until we finally gave in to what we suspected was our fate. Each other.

While on vacation Harris often called me from home. He was a worrier. Lord, if I didn't drive my car out of the garage fast enough, he would call me making sure no one had abducted me. I couldn't take our dog out after dark unless he accompanied me. He bought me high powered flashlights for my vehicle and pepper spray for my keychain.

Harris checked the locks on our doors twice and thrice. He made sure the curtains were closed before dark because there was a bus stop close to our apartment. I think you get my drift. Harris was obsessed with watching over me. He seemed fearful something terrible would happen to me. It truly wasn't normal, but I appreciated and tolerated it. For the most part, anyway.

I decided to share my findings with Harris by phone. Probably not the wisest decision I have ever made. And then in the middle of our conversation, the phone went dead. He said he tried to call back, but I was standing right by the phone and it never rang. I am not sure what happened, but I had a voice mail from Harris asking me why I didn't answer. What was happening? He had called! Who and what was messing with us?

And so, Harris arrived on the next flight in from our home State. And so goes my vacation. He had not disclosed his true concerns regarding my sharing Eden Barker's murder story with him. He just said he missed me and would see me soon. I was familiar with Harris's thinking process, but I was so enthralled in the old newspaper writings and what had transpired on the North Shore Beach I couldn't get past that experience. I should have caught it, but I did not. And so there he was on the beach and in the beach house with me and my hundred-year-old murder investigation.

It was the second night at the beach house Harris shared a startling revelation with me. Something I was not prepared to hear, nor did I know what to do with. Harris confided to me that when I initially told him about Eden and Johan on the beach, he experienced a moment in time that took him someplace he didn't understand. He told me he had a déjà vu moment.

My replay to Harris was an astounding, "WHAT?"

He told me he could feel everything those two kids and I had felt spiritually and physically. Like he had been given the same gift I was given that day. Or was my description so deeply vivid that he could feel it? Harris was not a "Nancy Boy!" He was black and white and no grey. And this was definitely a large, grey cliffhanger.

What could Harris have meant?

Chapter Three
Not-so-Quiet Time

This day found Harris and me going in different directions. Harris seemed to be driven toward finding more information on the young deceased couple than I was. I had come to this quiet village for some peace and quiet time away from the years of earthly muck. I believe that is why I became so engrossed – or rather "sidetracked" from my earthly life that I literally became one with two young deceased kids. There had to be a solid explanation for this strange occurrence.

I tried going shopping which usually held my attention very well but not this time. My mind continued churning mixed with voices coming through loud and sometimes clear. The one voice that wouldn't let up was the young man Johan's. At least, I assumed it was his voice. I tried with all had in me to rid myself of this assignment by the dead. But the dead refused to release me.

Have you ever heard a song that stayed with you an entire day into the night? The song ended in reality, but it continued in your head a thousand hundred times until you wanted to scream. Well, that is what was happening to me. And the words were very clear.

"Open the door; there is nothing to fear."

Open what door? I tried singing every song I could ever recall, but the voice drowned me out. I finally gave into it. I went back to North Shore Beach. I was walking toward the very spot I had encountered the two young deceased lovers. And it began again. I heard his voice louder than before saying, "Open the door. Open the door of your heart for me."

I began weeping uncontrollably. My soul ached for this boy Johan. I could feel his heart and mine were one. I felt his anguish, his yearning for me. But it wasn't for me; it had to be for Eden. Why was I feeling all his emotions for Eden so intensely? All I could think was I must be the only person who could release these two kids caught in some dream state unaware that they have died. They must be incapable of taking action toward a conscious level of awareness where they could direct themselves towards a higher plane of spirit.

Wait, me? Suddenly, I felt I was either giving myself way too much credit here, or I was that important in this insane scenario. Either one scared the bee-jee-bees out of me. I mean, there were times in my life I had experienced deja vu's wildly intense dreams and confusion about life and where we go after this train wreck of a life.

I had read the Bible, practiced serious prayer rituals, tried different religions, and rubbed the belly of Buddha, not to mention my many sins along the way. I wondered if they canceled out the good I had done. I have read books people have written after having an out of body experience during surgery or have literally died and come back to this life. The latest theory is, we are just in the other room. Yeah, right!

When Johan spoke to me, it did seem as though he were in the next room and only a thin veil kept us apart. The English Bible speaks of that veil between "Heaven" and

Earth. The Catholics believe it serious at death so the deceased can travel in the right direction.

If in life, the person had fear and chaos then in death that is the road they would be drawn to. Thus the prayers to help them onto an easier path for the next birth. An example of an attempt to create such a ritual is the Catholic rosary, where Mary as intercessor is requested to;

"Pray for us sinners, now and at the hour of our death."

That phrase is from the Hail Mary Prayer. It is believed by doing the rosary repetitively it will become mentally automatic and lead us out of confusion at the time of death.

As I stood weeping while overthinking what had transpired the last few days, the voice came again. This time stronger than the other times. And this time, I felt Eden's presence as well as Johan's pleading voice. Eden was encapsulated in death, and I was experiencing it. She had no feelings of anything earthly or spiritually. She was in a very dark prison of someone else's making.

No wonder Johan was begging for help. My tears were his tears. And those tears held words and emotions and colors I could feel with agonizing pleading. And so, through me, he was able to release some of the pain he had held for years while waiting for his Eden. I had to help him further, but I had no clue how. With all my years of wisdom, meditation, Church, and experiences, I had no clue how to help these two kids out of their prison of death. And so, we wept until I had no earthly tears left. I left Johan on the beach slumped over an imaginary clear casket that held his love, Eden.

I felt as though I were leaving my own self behind. The grief was unimaginable, and I could feel every stinging bite of it. Somehow, I had to control these borrowed emotions if I were to ever entertain any answers from the spirit or receive any earthly clues. Part of me actually thought I might be losing my mind. They say schizophrenics hear voices. Sometimes, they even kill people if the voices tell them to. So far, all I heard was a young man asking for help to find the killer of the love of his life, Eden. And that would release her from her spiritual coffin.

I was lost as to what to do next.

I am not sure why I didn't think of it sooner, but I suppose it was due to the overwhelming nature of the occurrence itself. I mean, who sees two dead people on a beach that no one else has seen in over a hundred years? Surely, Johan had tried to communicate with others. I decided I would ask him given the opportunity. And why didn't Johan know who killed them? Why was Eden the only one unable to communicate in the hereafter? Why wasn't Johan in the same untouchable death chamber as Eden was? And most of all why me? Why was I nominated kingdom cop and savior of the dead?

After days of research, I gave up on my quest to find a hundred-year-old murderer and turned to vacation mode with Harris.

And from that day on, neither Harris nor I mentioned our mental state of consciousness that plateaued us to the threshold of spiritual awareness of Johan and Eden in death. It was as if it never happened. Yet each of us carried a private mental detective search as to how and why those two dead kids were able to transmigrate through our minds here on earth.

Where is Harris anyway? I have been way too tied up in a dream that most likely isn't real anyway.

Chapter Four
Mickie and I

Harris

"Where is Mickie?"

Her given name is Michelle, but I have always referred to her as my Mickie. I hadn't seen her all day. And God and everyone else knows that I fret over her whereabouts and her wellbeing on a daily basis. Some say I should get some help, as in a therapist, but I figure I just love her more than most.

I do hope she ended up trying to figure out all those crazy voices she heard on the beach. Hellfire, she figures they were from the afterlife. Me, I figure we are born, live it out, and then pass on. Do the best we can and get buried in different kinds of dirt depending on our behavior during our earthly walk. I find it best not to share too much of my belief system with Mickie considering we differ in our hereafter beliefs. Sometimes, it's best just to bite my tongue. Until it bleeds, if necessary.

Mickie was born with a wild imagination as well as being one of the happiest people I have ever had the privilege of marrying. In fact, the only one. She could find something good in a man or woman who just robbed a bank, shot the teller, and he died. Me, I am more the impatient person always finding what the teller at the bank did wrong, and if he had done it right, he would still be alive. Or how anyone could do anything better than what I saw them do. Mickie always tried to convert me to a more positive, patient person. I guess we both figure we are too old to change now so we find the good in one another and try to let the rest go.

I will say I did sense something very strange when Mickie told me about those two dead kids on the beach. And I will say I wonder what that was about and why I felt as odd as in like the hair on the back of my neck and everywhere else was standing at military attention. Aw, I been around her too long. I figured her mental gears had rubbed off onto mine. Regardless, I let it all go. It was easier for me to do that than it was for Mickie. She had a one-track mind when she felt she was onto something. It was, get out of her way and now.

Mickie and I never brought up the kids on the beach for over a year. Every now and again, it would come into my mind, but I hesitated to bring it up. Mickie would have nightmares more often than I thought was normal. I would hold her as I ran my fingers through her beautiful soft sandy blonde hair at the same time reassuring her everything was fine. But she was so frightened. She claimed she could not recall any of the dreams. How could she be so terrified and not remember?

I never shared with Mickie that I had also entertained very strange dreams in the night. Nor did I share with her it was a reoccurring dream for me. The fact is I didn't share that with anyone. Anyway, who would I have told without looking like a complete psychological train wreck in need of a lobotomy? Nope, I kept the dream my dream. I did look up the definition of a dream. You know, just to see.

Dream: a series of thoughts, images, and sensations occurring in a person's mind during sleep.

I figured that seemed innocent enough. And so once again I let it all go until the next night when it hit me again. This time I woke up screaming.

Mickie was beside herself due to the fact I had never woke up screaming in all the time she had known me. Not even from the memories of war. No, I was terrified and running from a horrible, evil thing. I couldn't remember what it was except that I felt I had done something wrong. Never in my life had I experienced such fear. I was trembling as I perspired from every pore in my body. Mickie put her hands on both my shoulders shaking me to get me to come back to some sort of sanity. Why, I frightened the poor woman out of her wits. She was almost to the state I was in.

She got me a glass of water but instead of drinking it I bounded from the bed and ran straight to the liquor cabinet for a shot of Whiskey. And then another shot. At the third shot, Mickie took the bottle away while suggesting I sit down and breathe, which I did. She also brought me a heavy warm towel. I wanted to crawl inside that towel and stay forever. I didn't clearly understand why nor did she. I just wanted to hide where it was safe.

After I calmed down or after the whiskey hit, I was able to lean back on the sofa and relax with my towel. God, you'd have thought that towel was my mommy fifty years ago. Mickie calmly sat beside me and carefully asked me what happened. What did I dream?

I was afraid to tell her. So, I didn't.

Mickie and I had not had an easy life. Not before we met nor after. The fact is when Mickie left me after High School, I was irrationally angry. I wouldn't leave her alone. I followed her, I called her, and I stalked her until the law took over and made me stop. Another fact is I did some jail time for domestic abuse. I loved her so much I refused to let her go. I had experienced so much abandonment in my life I couldn't see the situation clearly.

As I look back, I understand why she was so frightened of me. But I had no notion of it back then. Mickie married another and moved far away from me. But in my mind, I thought she loved me and would love me forever. She did, but I had ruined it. I remember actually buying a gun with thoughts of harming both of us sort of immaturely like Romeo and Juliet.

But obviously, I didn't follow through with that nor did I ever share that with anyone. I rebounded and married one of Mickie's classmates. I didn't love her, but I stayed for the two children we had. I entered therapy for a couple of years trying to get all the unraveled string in my head put back together. Most of the time I felt like Humpty Dumpty. My marriage eventually dissolved.

I was walking toward the pharmacy in the small town I grew up in when I ran directly into Mickie walking toward me. We were thirty-five years older and likewise smarter. I invited her to have lunch with me, and she did. I still recall looking into her eyes and feeling the same love I felt all those years ago. And I could tell she was feeling something too. After that day, we reconnected and spent every possible moment together until this day. We never spoke of the turmoil I caused after our Teenage breakup.

I was from a very large family and she was from a small farm family. My parents divorced several times and then died. Hers stayed together in unhappiness then died. Our children all moved far away and the ones that didn't found reasons not to visit. There were a few Grandchildren but again they had moved to other parts of the country. We would take mini trips to visit them but never stayed too long. They say blended families take four years to blend. They lived too far away for blending time. There were also hurt feelings over divorces.

One of Mickie's sons was turned away from her due to the father's sharing of unkind words toward Mickie. And I had similar on my end. So, Mickie and I pretty much stayed to ourselves. A few cousins here and there, along with weddings and funerals. For some crazy reason, we liked to walk through cemeteries. Mickie always said she could think more clearly there. She also said she could hear from the dead. I, of course, discounted that due to my Bible teachings. I always told her she should be careful of who she was talking to. It could be the bad guy. But she usually did it anyway.

We liked to walk through antique stores. I would search out old coins and more old coins while Mickie would head right for the jewelry. She favored the old antique jewels versus the expensive diamonds at the corner Jewelry Store owned by the same family that owned the theater and the drug store. She always said to be careful as sometimes a person that has passed on can attach to an item. But not to worry she could pray them on their way.

Me, I didn't believe in such nonsense until one day it happened to me. We were walking through a maze of glass cases full of army paraphernalia when I experienced a spirit. Yes, siree. A strong one at that. It was a cold mist of anger that flashed past me or me past it whichever it was, it was. All I know is, I informed Miss Mickie that we were out of there – and now. Of course, she was tickled and boasted some about being right. I bit my tongue although there was no arguing as to what I experienced.

You see, the dream that frightened me to the point of feeling near death was similar to that angry cold spirit I felt at the antique store. It was nothing to laugh about. Once again, Mickie and I never shared what was happening to each of us separately. Little did we know more was to come and there would be no escape. No amount of whiskey would fix it.

Chapter Five
Déjà vu

Another six months passed with no shared discussion regarding the nightmares we were both experiencing. Mickie had sought out therapy but me? I believed I was strong enough to handle a few disturbing dreams. And so, we carried on each with our own professions as well as household chores, a movie, and out to eat with friends on occasion. Friends started to notice our relationship had become different. Not that we had any public disagreements, but we were not as loving and happy as we used to be. Mickie was always the life of any party so when her shining smile disappeared it was truly noticeable. I myself was beginning to feel the strain on our marriage.

My negative feelings were nagging at both of us. Those feelings and the dreams brought with them more hurtful thoughts. Without talking about what was going on inside of us the split continued to grow. Our togetherness, our being one was more like a separate two most of the time. Yet both of us not able to open the forbidden door of our/my nightmares, mostly because we didn't understand the dreams were the problem, or so we thought.

We had built a wall between us, and it was devouring us from the inside. We used to write beautiful love letters to each other. Send cards for no reason. And always touch or brush against one another as we passed in the hallway or kitchen. "It" whatever "it" was had triggered a hidden sadness and fear in our lives. An uncertainty neither of us could pinpoint. And again, nothing was discussed. We were lost as to know what to even discuss.

Mickie hadn't returned from work that Thursday, and I was beginning to get concerned. I was always overly concerned about Mickie's well-being. For some unknown reason, I feared something happening to her. Yes, even feared I would lose her to death. I couldn't explain my irrational uneasiness. Mickie always said it was because I had been abandoned by so many people I loved. I took her word for it because I surely never loved anyone like I loved Mickie. And so, that was how I rationalized my odd behavior.

But now it was two hours past time for her to be home. Even though I knew she had a therapy appointment after work she should have been home long ago. She would have called me had she decided to stop anywhere else. Now it was three hours and I was about ready to start driving around town searching for my wife. At four hours I was pacing and had imagined all the worst-case scenarios.

I knew if I called the police with a missing person's report, they would laugh privately at the husband missing his wife for a mere four hours. So, I got the phone book out and was about to start calling the only two hospitals in our city to see if she had been in an accident when the front doorbell rang. I was so relieved thinking Mickie had lost her keys and was finally home, I ran not walked to the door. I flung it open in grand but nervous anticipation only to see two police officers standing before me.

I know my face turned white because I could feel all my blood leave my upper body and descend to my feet. That is when I started to collapse. The two officers caught me going down and basically dragged me to the sofa where each sat on either side of me while waving some God-awful smelling thing under my nose. When I came back to half-life, I immediately started yelling, "What happened to Mickie?" Screaming, asking if she were dead.

"Mr. Jeffers, take a deep breath, sir, your wife has been in a serious car accident on the West Beltway. She has been transported by ambulance to St. John's University Hospital in Gainesville. Do you have someone that can drive you? You are in no condition to drive, sir. We will stay with you while you call someone."

I was so frantic I couldn't remember my own phone number much less my buddy Stan's number. I excused myself to the kitchen, opened the liquor cabinet, downed two shots of whiskey, leaned on the cupboard for thirty seconds hoping it would hit fast. One of the officers walked into the kitchen to check on me at which time I handed him our local phone book while giving him Stanley's first and last name. He found the number for me as well as dialed it up.

"Stan, Harris here. Mickie was in a terrible car accident. I don't have any details yet. Only that she is at St. Johns and I need you to come get me and take me to her. I am unable to drive."

I turned to the officers informing them my friend was on his way and that I would be okay until he arrived. I hoped they would leave because I would have jumped in my car and driven to that hospital like a man terrified of losing his wife to the next phase called death. But they refused to go until Stan arrived.

I thought we would never get to the hospital. Stan drove every speed limit like the honest citizen he was. I was pushing him with words, hand motions, and some cursing, but he ignored me and drove on at a steady pace.

I still had no details. My mind was taking me places it shouldn't have. I had my wife dead and buried, and I was grieving when I flew open the emergency room doors.

"Where's my wife?" I was not using my inside voice that was for sure.

The woman at the desk calmly asked me what my wife's name was. I did not respond with the courtesy she had bestowed upon me. I shouted at her in anger. This time, she hit a button that called security. I suspect I frightened her. The immediate thought that came to me was all the times Mickie informed me that, when I got angry like that, I frightened her also.

I apologized to the nurse at the desk and calmly said, "Michelle Jeffers."

She instructed the two security officers to escort me to room 9.

I could hear a lot of commotion as I neared room 9. When I looked through the window there were four doctors, two nurses, and my wife, unrecognizable and covered in blood. I walked in only to be promptly but kindly ushered back out of the room.

"Mr. Jeffers? I am Doctor Friedland."

"Yes, that is my wife; I need to tell her I'm here. I need to touch her. I need to tell her I love her, doctor."

"Mr. Jeffers, we are doing everything we can for your wife. I will tell her you are here, although she is unconscious, and we have intubated her as her lungs were collapsed. So far, we have also determined she may have a severe concussion along with minor lacerations that need attention as well. Someone will come and get you as soon as your wife's condition is stabilized."

I recall asking that doctor if my wife was going to survive or what her chances were. He responded with a somber 50/50. And told me the Chapel was down the hall on the left.

I stood outside her room staring at the woman I loved with all my life. The words that came out of my mouth to God were, "If she dies God, I will die with her." At that moment Stan took my arm and gave me enough strength to walk to the Chapel where I sat staring at the picture of the man on the cross that died for my sins. I couldn't think of one word to say or pray. I was numb with fear, irrational fear. And at that very moment, something happened in my head, and I was living somewhere else other than the Chapel. It was a reflective deja'vu moment.

I was experiencing myself witnessing the second death of my wife. I was living two occasions of the same crisis. I was questioning where I was, which time I lived in. I seemed to be in a period of introspection where old memories reappeared from the past. And then I snapped out of it. But I didn't forget what I had just felt, lived, and seen. Whatever just happened would stay with me forever as well as change our lives. And I was sure it was not the whiskey.

Stan was shaking me and then shaking me harder. I heard him say, "Man, what the hell? What are you sorry for? You didn't do anything? Come on buddy, snap out of it! We haven't lost her. She'll make it?"

I was sobbing and mumbling uncontrollably. Later, Stan asked me why I kept repeating I was sorry for hurting Mickie. I responded telling him he must have misunderstood me because I had no idea why I would say such a thing. I thought I was simply delusional due to the stress of my wife possibly dying and thinking that, if I had been with her, this may not have happened.

Chapter Six
Dreams and Visions

Mickie remained in the hospital for three weeks. I was irrationally out of my mind at times with her gone. I felt like she was never coming home even though the doctors assured me she was mending well and not to worry. They actually asked me if I had contacted my local General Practitioner for, well, maybe a prescription to calm me down. God, I was so crazy acting, the hospital staff noticed it. Yet I refused to get any outside help. I was distraught with unreasonable delusional fears. My nightmares had gotten worse since Mickie's accident. I would see her dead and me kneeling over her saying I was sorry over and over. Why was I seeing that? And how could I ever share that with anyone? Ever!

I was missing work because I wasn't sleeping. I was terrified to go to sleep on the grounds, afraid that if I did, I would have to see my wife dead. Each night, it was getting worse.

Stan stopped over to check on me one evening after work. When I opened the door the look on his face gave me away. He pushed his way inside, looked at me sternly, and said.

"Mickie is fine, Harris, so what in the hell is going on with you? You look like death has visited you! We need to talk, my friend."

"Just go, Stan. I will be fine. I just miss my wife!"

"No way, Harris. This is more than just missing your wife. You have all the signs of having a mental breakdown. Why? Let me help you. Should I call your mother or your sister? This is serious, Harris. Anyone can see that except you. Why, if Mickie were to be released from the hospital tomorrow, you wouldn't be in any condition to care for her. She mentioned to my wife how concerned she is about you. You're stressing her out, Harris. It's time to get some help."

"Get out, Stan. Get out!"

I pushed Stan backward until he fell and hit his head on the planter by the door. He rolled over to get up, but I stood over him, screaming over and over that I was sorry; I didn't mean to kill him. Stan got up, ran out my front door to his car, and drove away like a scared child. But me, I just walked into the kitchen and poured myself another whiskey, hoping to regain my mental faculties. And then I slept until the nightmares came back with a vengeance. I was losing my mind and unsure how to stop it or where to go or whom to tell.

Sometimes, the body just gives up. The organs can't go on without sleep, and so I slept for many hours with no interruption until I heard my doorbell ring. I was so angry at the thought of Stan coming back and waking me up, I flew toward the front door, hollering like the crazy man I had become at whoever was on the other side of that door. I flung it open as I said, "What the hell do......"

My sister calmly looked at me... no, she stared at me for what seemed like an eternity. Then she asked me if I was going to invite her in. I told her no, I wasn't, and furthermore, Stan had no business calling her. I was fine.

She sarcastically agreed, commenting on how amazing I looked indeed.

"Black circles under your eyes, sunken cheeks, the next thing to matted hair, and a temperament likened to the devil himself. And by the way, Stan did not call me, Mickie did. She is very concerned about you. I was going to come down and visit both of you anyway because Mom gave me a box of photos from her Aunt Gusty she believed might interest you. She has been working on our family history and wanted to share it. There are some interesting facts in here, Harris. Oh, and some photographs of our ancestors too. I had no idea we came from the United Kingdom. I always thought we hailed from Norway or Sweden. Guess not. Now, back to you, brother dear. Let me fix you something decent to eat while you go get yourself a good, hot, relaxing shower. Everything is going to be just fine; you'll see."

I just stood there, actually thankful Beulah had come down from the city. For some reason, the fear that had been trapped inside me seemed to dwindle some. I went for the hot shower. Yes, she was right; everything would get back to normal now. My sister always had a way of taking care of me. Even though I was the oldest, she was the nurturer.

And so, we had a nice dinner, then we went through some of Mother's findings on our family tree. That was the calmest I had felt in weeks… actually, come to think of it, since the trip to Enaid City and that damn North Shore Beach vision of Mickie's. I began to wonder if some sort of demonic entity had come over me. But, of course, no one would believe that one. Not even me, nor did I share such idiocy with anyone.

Beulah was laying out what seemed like a hundred photos on the kitchen table, while I was reading Mom's notes. And then there it was. A photo of a young man sitting and a pretty girl standing behind him. There was a newspaper article attached with a common pin through both the photo and the newsprint to make sure they stayed together in that box, and they had for a hundred plus years.

Beulah handed it across the table to me, so I took it from her, and as I did, I saw the headline. "The Murder of Eden Barker." It told how she was strangled to death by her lover, Johan, and her body was later found on the North Shore Beach in Enaid City. The young couple hailed from the United Kingdom. The young woman was a nurse, her boyfriend unemployed. No reason was given for her murder other than it was a suspected murder-suicide.

Beulah stood up, eyes big as saucers, and said, "Harris, what the hell, Harris? You are white as a ghost. Come on, I am taking you to the hospital. Come on NOW!"

But I refused to go. I told Beulah I was pretty sure I had the flu and, in fact, needed to go throw up! And at that point, I ran to the upstairs bathroom and threw up all that dinner my sister had prepared and then some.

I had seen a ghost story – a real ghost story – and I was terrified to the moon. In fact, a trip to the moon would have been easier. I gathered myself as best I could and asked Beulah if she would mind going to visit Mickie for me. I surely didn't want to go to the hospital and get anyone sick. She agreed and left – after making me some tea with honey. But I knew tea and honey weren't going to cure what was ailing me. I was sure I had become possessed by the spirit of Johan Cline. Or was I him reborn?

Is that why I was having reoccurring dreams of standing over my wife's dead body? I must have dreamed or relived that murder what seemed like a thousand times, and it was killing me. Was this my penance? Or was I living his?

I recall Mickie sharing with me about her vision on the beach. How the young ghost had asked Mickie for help releasing his love, Eden, from her eternal grave. I could feel the young man's emotions then, and I could feel them now. I perceived he had been driven to the edge of any sense of reason on earth or the beyond. Thus, he was a "crisis apparition!"

Why did Mickie feel it? Why was I feeling it? Oh, dear God. Who are we? Is that why I am so afraid of something happening to Mickie… because it did? I never believed in such nonsense. I just needed to rest. But rest never came.

Chapter Seven
The Murder of Eden Barker

Mickie

"Hi, Beulah. So nice of you to visit me, it has gotten to be quite a long, boring hospital stay for me."

It was so nice to see Harris's sister. She was careful with her words, but I knew she was interrogating me delicately about Harris's actions and appearance lately. I agreed he had not been himself for quite some time, but I believed he would be fine once I was home again and got things back to some sense of normalcy.

But Beulah wasn't so sure, and as the conversation continued, she wasn't so careful with her wordings. She came right out and said she felt Harris was losing his mind and that I needed to be careful around him as he was not himself at all. I was a bit taken back by that statement, considering Beulah always had Harris's back.

In fact, when we were kids and he was out of control after we broke up, Beulah blamed me for everything that happened. Harris was Mr. Perfect in her eyes. Even when the law found him guilty of stalking and put him in jail, she stood by his side, defending him. But here she was, several decades later, warning me to beware of her brother. It was definitely an unsettling visit for both of us.

I told Beulah I was to be released at the end of the week. She said she would try to get back down and stay with us for a bit until my health was back to normal. I thanked her and actually was relieved, considering her cautioning statements.

I didn't tell her, but Stan's wife had also come to me regarding the incident at the house between Harris and Stan. She had told me how Harris had pushed Stan down in an aggressive manner and how Harris stood over Stan repeating how sorry he was for killing him. I was quite taken aback, wondering if possibly Stan misunderstood Harris's words, or maybe his brain was dimmed when he hit his head on the planter.

And once again, I dismissed Harris's actions as normal stress in light of my recent accident. If I had truly faced reality, I would have recalled how similar this was to his actions as a teenager. I knew he had been having disturbing dreams. He didn't admit to that, but I could tell. Sometimes, he would talk in his sleep, and other times, he would whimper like a boy.

I had some riveting dreams also, but nothing compared to what I felt Harris was experiencing. And it did seem like Harris's personality was changing, now that I thought on it. But what was I to do? Beulah's warning. Stan's wife's warning. The nightmares. Our past. I never dreamed Harris would regress, but perhaps I needed to heed the warnings. But how?

I was released from the hospital the following week. Harris was overly attentive to my every need at first. Beulah was unable to stay with us due to a serious case of the flu. And with each passing day, I was losing my confidence in the Harris I had married. Rather, I was seeing the troubled boy I knew in our youth.

Beulah was right; Harris wasn't himself. He seemed frightened all the time, like someone or some danger was around every corner. He jumped at the slightest noise; he had no patience for even the smallest inconvenience. Harris hadn't shouted at me since we reconnected later in life… that is, until now. In fact, I was beginning to sense a fear of him. How could this be? I loved Harris with all my heart and soul. And then it happened.

It had been a normal Sunday. We had gone to church, which we had not done for a long time. I thought it would help Harris to restore his faith in God. And he seemed fine with going, not realizing I had a secret motive for initiating it. He even smiled a few times and made a joke or two.

We went out for dinner and then home for a nap. I had noticed his drinking of whiskey had accelerated to a level not appropriate, but I said nothing. It had gotten to the place I felt I was walking on eggshells around Harris. I lay down on our bed to nap when Harris came into the room.

He smelled of strong whiskey, but again, I said nothing. He lay next to me. Harris was the man I loved beyond the moon, but that man was not lying next to me. It was someone else. Not knowing what to say or do at that moment, I drifted off to sleep.

I awoke to Harris's shrieking at me, his face and eyes the color red. He had his hands around my neck, and as I screamed, he tightened his grip. Surely, the fear in my eyes should have stopped him, but it did not. I could no longer scream. I recall seeing hundreds of shining stars, and at the same time, I saw Eden Barker and felt Eden dying as I was dying. The terror in your heart, mind, and body when you cannot breathe and know you are dying has no earthly description. It is the end. And that is when I passed out... or died... I knew not which.

I could still hear Harris's sobs in between his crazy apologies for killing me. But what I actually saw in my death – or out of body experience – was Johan. Johan standing over me, begging me to help him release the love of his life from her prison of darkness. Eden did not want to go with Johan to any other dimension after their deaths. Eden did not want to be with Johan. He had murdered her and was delusional that she still loved him in death. Harris had taken on Johan's spirit. Yes, he had become possessed by the murderous demon.

Even in my darkness, I could now see the truth that had remained hidden for a hundred years but came back to life through the rebirth of Johan and Eden as Harris and Mickie. Harris could have changed history, but he did not have the strength to stand up and fight. Neither for his love nor for himself.

Harris snapped, but he also snapped out of his possessed state of mind after he believed he had killed me. Harris called the local constable and was arrested. He had no idea I survived his and Johan's Murder of Eden Barker.

I was once again hospitalized until my injuries healed. I never spoke to Harris again in his lifetime. I never again had any nightmares where I was being murdered. I never again heard from Johan Cline, who never took responsibility for his crime but will now through Harris.

But I did hear from Eden Barker. When my Harris was possessed by Johan, strangling me, and I was dying, Eden appeared to me, smiling. And then I saw Eden's spirit release from Johan's evil grip and ascend to heaven. She had been freed through the reincarnation, life, and in the end, the spiritual death of Johan's inability to accept and or take responsibility for her murder.

After going through such a harrowing experience and losing my husband, I did some research. The soul is many times caught in a dream state, unaware that it has died and incapable of taking action to raise its state of consciousness to a level of awareness where it can direct its attention towards spiritual states. I believe that is what happened to Johan Cline.

Beulah asked for my forgiveness. I in turn passed on to Harris's children the box of photos and information on their heritage from Harris's mother. I took out the photo and newspaper clipping about The Murder of Eden Barker. And then I changed my mind and put it back in the box. I have learned our ancestor's cells have memories, and in my life, I had given the unacceptable cells an open door through Harris. I hoped the future generations would heed the demon of murder in their family box of "the way we were." Or "our generational curses."

In the end, I was released from Harris's Earthly demons he allowed from his past generational curses. Godspeed and wisdom because we all must learn not to entertain the wolf in the sheep's clothing.

About the Author

Julianna Rowe is truly a gifted writer of fiction because of her gift of imagination. She is a spiritual person, also. So, coupled with her imagination comes wisdom and insight into the enjoyment of other humans, the people who also possess the kind of fear that seems to excite the emotions, and yet they cling to a logical outcome to her stories. Those conclusions don't leave the readers cringing in fear. Instead, they leave the reader excited; yet satisfied.

Julianna is a prolific writer in many different literary genres. In all of her writing, her descriptive words transport the reader directly into the stories, making them part of the literary scenario which completely captures their interest until the end.

The Way It Was Told
Katie Jaarsveld

It was hearsay. He said, she said, and so on. It started
with the lives of the tiniest things.

It was on a lonely, tearful walk when I tripped over a tree root, then did a face-plant in the moist soil. I heard chatter unlike any noise I'd ever heard. I lifted my head to see a light, and it was coming from inside the trunk of the tree. I peered into the knothole when the tip of my nose was poked by something sharp, and extremely unpleasant in odor.

"You think the gunk on your face smells pleasant? It's the same horrific odor, thank you very much." She sounded a bit snooty.

I looked around and not one person was to be seen. I pressed on the tree for balance to stand, and my hand felt a pinch. I jerked it away and almost fell back in the soil.

"So now you tried to squish us as well as eavesdrop and interrupt our important meeting? We are on such a strict schedule. These interruptions simply cannot be allowed to continue."

My revised opinion was, she was bossy, rude, demanding, with an air of authority and—. My thoughts were interrupted as my hand was pricked again.

"If you would hush, you would be allowed to stay. Otherwise, I'll have to banish you."

"Banish me?" Now it was my turn to get a little attitude. "You think you can banish me from the forest? Great! Another place I'm not wanted, and on my birthday, too." I could feel the tears well up. I really did not want to cry in front of whoever or whatever she was.

I felt nauseous and itchy. All I needed on top of everything else was poison ivy. My clothes felt tight, then loose, really loose. When I struggled free, I found myself still clothed, minus my shoes and coat.

"That apparel is tragic, but we will have to make do. We can't hold the conference up any longer." She shrieked, "Someone, swear this creature in and gather a drop of blood for truth."

"My blood will say what's true?" I felt another prick and stuck my finger to my mouth.

"Vile creatures, licking their bloody wounds. Of course, it won't, silly child. Us having your blood, all our blood, keeps us honest. No one can tell even what you would call a white lie. From what I've seen of your race, you could learn from us."

I nodded yes. "I agree on that point," I stated simply.

She looked shocked. "There may be hope for you at least, then." With a harrumph, she told someone to seat me, then I was brought cookies and hot tea with milk.

I hadn't noticed until then that I was smaller. For some reason, it mattered not. I looked straight ahead and saw one of my shoes leaning against the tree. I suppressed a giggle.

She continued speaking without an introduction, glancing my way as if to silence me.

"I am Aziza. It is the name of my people, and as their leader, my name was changed to reflect with honor on us. As many here are, so my African tribe is also generous and believes in doing good deeds. As a fae, with humanoid features but with wings, we also resemble a butterfly.

"We have helped hunters with our magic, with fire and their techniques in hunting. But we will not help any who would cause us grief. I would like the rest of the council to introduce themselves. While I recognize your species, I'm not familiar with all of the names of new faces."

Another winged spirit stood and while others gasped at her beauty, I was surprised I understood what she said when she started speaking.

"I am Peri, and I am a fairy. We are known among Persian and Armenian cultures, among others. We are mother-like creatures who assist those with good hearts. Where there are nature and fruit are where we can be found. We also tend to be mischievous, which is our undoing as we have been denied entry into any paradise for a time until we have completed so much penance for atonement."

As soon as Peri sat, another stood. His voice was raspy with wisdom and age.

"I am Tien." He bowed at the waist to Aziza with his hands clasped in front of me, and she returned the gesture. Obviously, they were acquainted. "My people are considered to be heavenly beings in Vietnam. We are in the same classification as immortals, spirits, fairies, and angels."

He bowed and sat down, replaced in standing by a beautiful fairy woman.

"I am Sidhe, a supernatural being from Ireland. We women are female spirits, occasionally referred to as banshees. No males are born to us, so our mates are human. It does not reflect on the children for us to have human males."

An elf stood, and even I recognized him. I had seen a picture of him in mom's belongings.

"I am Armin, we are the first of the eight families of fairy people, according to the Germanic records.

"As long as I can remember there have always been elves, fairies, dwarfs, dragons, griffins, mermaids, giants, gnomes, trolls, goblins, faeries, sprites, and talking animals. While some are vile, some became brethren over time. We don't need to be blood to be family, but we must honor and respect each other for whatever we are."

Aziza was nodding her head yes, and I didn't miss when a tear slid down her cheek to form a crystal in the palm of her hand. She looked at me with a sad smile as another tear slid down her face. She shook her head no and waited for Armin to take a seat.

As Armin seated himself and picked up his teacup, two beings came through the knothole.

A beautiful, young girl, and a male who walked upright on two legs like I do, but with hoofed legs.

"I am a nymph, Alkyi, and considered an inferior divinity, though I have no ideas as to why. Our people are Greek in origin and help things which grow, such as trees. We are not immortal, but we do have a lengthy lifespan. We are female spirits of nature. If a tree were to die that I am attached to, I would cease to exist, and my body would become a part of the tree that I inhabit."

"I am a satyr, Maysyr, also Greek, and most of my kind spend our lives trying to get a nymph. We were born for entertaining, partying, and known for our animalistic ways. I am part man, part horse. We are fertility spirits."

He was stunning is what he was, and nude. Thick curls on his head, a beard that flowed down his chest, short horns, long and pointed ears. His tail was magnificent, sweeping to the ground.

Aziza looked over and me, and I could swear she was blushing. Was she reading my mind? She winked at me. Now it was my turn to blush.

"We also have a hunger for things and don't take 'no' for an answer. Sadly, in the past, we have been responsible for less than gentlemanly behavior with nymphs and mortals. We have calmed over centuries with our music. When we have our wild parties and brawls, it's away from those we care for."

He looked at the nymph with a caring beyond love and understanding. I had never felt more alone. I didn't see the next one, but I heard her.

"I am Alux, a sprite from the Yucatan Peninsula. I am here in my father's stead. We are virtually immortal, also indestructible. I have mastered the skills for the craft of illusion."

When she moved, I saw her. She had pointed ears and looked like a miniature mortal. Her wings looked like a combination of a dragonfly and a butterfly since you could see the veins in the wings. She hovered in the air, just above where others sat.

Water sprayed through the knothole in the tree, and she flew behind me, to the back of the tree, and shook her wings dry.

"I am Encantado, Portuguese and come from the Encante, an underwater paradise of shapeshifters, spirit beings, on to dolphins and we all have the ability to turn to mortal and back to our natural forms."

As he was speaking, I saw two males that I had not noticed before. There was one standing to each side of the knothole. When Encantado moved to the side, these males stood side by side and blocked the knothole.

When they spoke, they spoke in unison, in deep, booming voices.

"We are Curupira, supernatural guards of the forest and regarded as demonic figures when in reality, we are protectors in the forests of Brazil."

They looked at each other, changed sides then continued. I didn't hear what they said, if they said anything. I was looking at their feet, which were backward. Their hair was fire red/orange, and looking at them one time they looked mortal, and in another instant, they looked to be dwarf.

"We use our feet to create a confusing point for hunters or travelers since they're backwards. We can create illusions, also whistle in a high pitch to scare our victims or drive them mad, whichever comes first. Anyone who hunts animals who are taking care of their offspring, we attack."

They looked back at each other, traded sides, then went back to guarding the knothole.

The room became silent after their last statement, and the loud voices being silenced. Even Aziza was shocked into silence. She cleared her voice and stood.

"As some of you may have noticed, we have a mortal here, which has never been done in our history."

Some were looking around, but no one looked *at* me. I looked at me and noticed that I was a bit shorter and smaller than most present. Aziza stood and walked over to where I sat. I felt smaller and hugged my knees to my chest.

"This child was found outside this very tree, in tears. She has no one who wants her. As many of you know, my life has been to protect this very council. I never took a mate or had a family of my own. If this conference does not disagree, I would take her as my own."

I looked up at her, amazed someone wanted me. No one had ever wanted me; in fact, most had ignored me, treated me as invisible, or left me.

"Child. You can go if family comes to look for you – if you choose."

"The way it was told to me repeatedly, I wasn't wanted." I felt the tears well up and tried to talk them out of falling, but two escaped, and Aziza caught them on her fingers.

"In our family, you are cherished."

One by one, the council stood and agreed, even the Curupira.

Aziza had me stand. I hadn't noticed the back of my shirt being torn on both sides. She held up her hand and showed my tears. With her other hand, she fished something out of her pocket... her tears, which turned to crystals. Aziza put it all in one hand, and Alux flew over to me, saying words I didn't understand.

Everyone was humming a beautiful tune that was hypnotic. Aziza went behind me, while Alux held my gaze.

"This will be the most painful thing you have ever felt, mortal child, but after this, you will be forever changed."

I didn't have time to ask any questions, for as soon as she had stopped speaking, I felt a pain so intense that it enveloped my whole body. All I heard was the humming. I couldn't even hear my own heartbeat. I couldn't see Alux. All I saw was a blinding light, a kaleidoscope of colors.

Members of the council were coming to me, one by one, even the Curupira. They kissed my forehead, then touched the spot they had kissed. Afterword, they all went behind me to Aziza.

There was a flood of memories, reflections of history from long ago. I was seeing and feeling emotions from an era I didn't know that I couldn't have known. Alux kissed my forehead, touched it, then went to Aziza. Aziza came and stood in front of me. She took my head in her hands and kissed my forehead, then pricked her finger and put it to my forehead.

Had they all pricked their fingers? Was I covered in blood from all of these creatures?

Aziza smiled a knowing smile and nodded yes. She picked up my finger, pricked it, and bled it into a cup. The blood still on my finger, she put to my forehead. The cup was passed among the council, with each member dipping a feather into it, and brushing it onto their foreheads.

It was strange. I knew my blood was in the cup, their feather contained red blood, and yet, there was no blood on their faces. My finger didn't hurt from being pricked, and there was no blood.

Aziza gazed at me, curious and confused.

"You shall be called, Jasy. Do you not feel pain or burning? Anything negative?"

"I feel strong actually and wanted. It's an odd feeling. My back feels tight."

I shrugged my shoulders and moved my back muscles. There was a breeze coming from behind me. Aziza and the others had an incredulous expression on their faces. Alux flew behind me. It felt as if she was tickling me.

I turned around too fast and saw her, literally flying across the room as if she had been tossed. A Curupira caught her.

"What's going on? Alux what happened?"

She shook her head no in disbelief. I expected more people to look behind me, but they actually stayed in front of me.

"I think she had a bit much from us. That's too powerful." One stated.

Others agreed or voiced an opinion.

Alux took my hand and drew me outside. I expected my coat and shoes to be there, but they were gone. It didn't matter, I wasn't cold anymore.

I could hear the water running through at the edge of the forest. Alux held my hand as we walked to the water. Aziza and the others were following. At the embankment's edge, there were creatures gazing at us, rippling the water. Alux shooed them off.

"Look, Jasy. You've changed." Alux encouraged me in her tiny voice, almost a whisper.

I looked down into the deep water, then knelt in front of it, leaning over. I didn't understand the reflection staring back at me. My long hair was pulled up in a high ponytail, with a braid wrapped around the hair by my head, holding it in place. It was now fire-red hair, not a mousy brown.

My face looked more mature, though there were still freckles on my nose. My eyes were a vibrant blue, no longer a dull, lifeless look of no color. I started to turn toward Alux, and I lost my balance, falling. And then I wasn't. I turned to thank whoever stopped me from falling the ten feet into the water, but no one was standing near me.

Alux flew to me and turned me so I saw the reflection of my side in the water. My mouth flew open, and I didn't have any words to explain all the questions forming in my head. In all actuality, no words were forming there either.

Aziza came up to me.

"You are now a part of the council and everyone present. We have all gifted you with a part of ourselves. I don't know if you will be immortal, or live for a long time, but you are virtually indestructible. It's important for you to do good deeds and assist those with good hearts. You were already mischievous, in challenging me, so that should be interesting.

"You will be capable of shapeshifting, using illusion, as well as the dreaded whistle. The magic will be powerful, but part of doing good will be to provide fire and improving hunting techniques for those who need the food, not for the sport."

I sneezed and Aziza flew backwards. I felt a hard wind, but when I took a deep breath, it stopped.

"Jasy, you're seriously going to have to get control of your wings before you blow us all away." Alux looked like she was half-teasing, but her eyes said she was serious."

"I'm sorry. I didn't realize that was me." I looked down, but Peri came and offered support.

"All you have to do is allow your instincts to help you. Like you just did. Take a deep breath when it feels like too much. It will calm you, and whatever you are doing at the moment. But, if you hold your breath, it will increase negativity. Negative energy may be stronger in some aspects, but believe me when I tell you that it's harder to control, and easier to use in bad ways, which in turn will destroy not only you but us as well because we are now all connected.

I asked for some time alone. Alux asked if she could stay with me, and I agreed. The rest went back to the conference.

I was thinking about me and how things were now when we heard people talking.

"Who knows where that girl went? Why are we looking for her? Do we really care? Her having telepathy was irritating, there was no privacy, not to mention her being an empath. Her stupid witch of a mother."

So, it wasn't that Aziza could read my thoughts, it was that we could read each other's. I never knew my mother, as she died right after giving birth to me. Something my father blamed me for. He wanted her, and not me to survive. He met this woman with sons and introduced them to me a week before my sixteenth birthday. Hell started the day after. He would never have married her, but he never wanted me either. It took a week for me to leave, right after *she* told me I would never amount to anything, and that I was never wanted, and never would be wanted.

That's how I ended up here.

I had powers. I could teach them a lesson, or at least blow them away. I remembered Peri's words. I could never hurt the council in any way.

The boys found my coat in the water and fished it out.

"Looks like the witch is dead. Mom will celebrate tonight. Her dad probably will too."

I felt the anger rise in me, and wings started to flutter furiously. The wind picked up, and I saw red. I took a deep breath, careful not to hold it, then released it. I had a lot of work to do in learning how to use my powers. But this was a start.

Tomorrow, I would start learning how to control my wings, then the rest of the powers.

Alux and I flew slowly back to the tree with the knothole. I was welcomed like I had always hoped to be welcomed by family. With hugs and love.

On to a new beginning...

About the Author

Katie started by writing horror, and though that is still her favorite genre, she has also released stories in contemporary, paranormal, supernatural, fantasy, mythopoeia, young adult, and even romance.

Twitter: @katiejaarsveld
Facebook: https://www.facebook.com/marytink.w

A Life in Review
Luna Black

As an author, I have faced many challenges, and there are many still come. I know that each road leads to a new destination. It was meant for me to be at this store for a book signing because the young teen that was about to enter the store would change my life for the better.

It was a sunny day as Oklahoma City Mall was busier than ever. I thought it would be a silent day, but boy, was I was wrong. I had no idea what would happen. My editor and proofreader were laughing as I set up the stand, trying not to think of what would happen if everything went wrong. You could say that I was nervous. I knew that I was, but I also knew that life would always keep me on my toes. I could not help but to laugh when I looked over at my friends. They are not just my coworkers and boss. They are my best friends.

My mother and daughter are the back, and for once, my daughter is being good. I chuckled at my thought. As I finished setting up and making sure that everything was right, I saw a young girl looking scared and worried as kids passed her and pointed and laughed. My heart stopped, and I could not help but get mad.

I looked at Lizzy and Katie. "Hey, guys, I am going to step outside real fast," I told them. They both nodded and went back to talking. I noticed that the kids who were laughing were sitting in the front row. My blood boiled as I stormed out of the building and up to the little girl crying.

"Are you okay? I saw those kids laughing at you. What is wrong?" I asked as I noticed that she reminded me of who I use to be.

She looked up and gasped. "You're the famous author, Luna Black," she stated, shocked.

I smiled at her. "Shhh, let's keep it between us."

She returned the smile and nodded. "Now, tell me, what were they making fun of you for? It's okay, you can tell me."

She took a deep breath. "Well, you see, I have been having seizures, and everyone just found out. They think it's funny. I really want to be a writer like you," she stated. I try to hide the tears as I look at her with a smile on my face.

"Listen, let's go get a drink, and I will tell you my life story on how I became who I have become." She smiled and followed me. "It was years ago, and everything started in Elementary school. I was made fun…"

She gasped as she looked at me. "You were made fun of? That cannot be true. You're one of the best authors around."

I laughed as she looks at me as if I have grown two heads. I cannot believe I am about to go back and relive the pain of the past, but maybe it will help the little girl. I take a deep breath and give her my best smile.

"Yes, I was bullied, many of my classmates hated me. I am just like you. I am human too. I have what they call a seizure disorder, epilepsy. I have had it since I was born. On top of that, try being made fun of for not being able to spell because your letters switch on you. I know that being Dyslexic is nothing major to a lot of people, but me? I hated it. I thought that God hated me for so long because, no matter how hard I tried, I always messed up. I remember one day, I was in class, and we were having a spelling test. It was like midterms, and it was the hardest test I had taken."

She looked at me and tried to hold tears back. I smiled at her and sighed. "It's okay. I knew that day that I would fail the test. Everyone knew that I would fail. As the teacher passed out the papers, she smiled at me and nodded. She knew that this would be hard, but I did not want to be treated like I was different. I knew for me to pull this off and make everyone believe in me, I had to pass that stupid test."

She looked at me as though she knew that feeling well.

I continued, "I looked down and tried so hard to remember everything that I had studied. I knew that I had studied for it. So, I focused as hard as I could. I put all my energy into what I was doing, and for once, my own mind changed. For the first time, I started writing the words correctly. I was so shocked. After the test, I just looked at the wall, not able to believe my own eyes. The teacher sat at her desk and started grading it. She did not expect anything more than the usual grades… mostly C's and a couple of B's. You see, this was a very difficult test. No one had ever gotten an A. Even the smartest kid in school missed two or three. We all sat waiting, but none of them was not worried like I was. They were more concerned with talking to their friends and making fun of me. I had something to prove."

The teacher walked from behind her desk twenty-five minutes later. She smiled at me, saying, 'Today, kids, we have a new record, and I want everyone to stand up and give Luna a big congratulations. She is the first student to ever get a 100 on this test.' As she spoke, I could not believe my ears. Yes, I was challenged, but that day, I knew that I had a fighting chance in this world."

She looked at me in awe. "But as much as you needed to hear that, I always want you to know that was not the end of my pain. As I got older, it got worse. The teasing was more hurtful. I was pushed and was the laughing joke of the school. In fourth grade, they had a writing contest. I was so excited, but my classmates tried to talk my teacher out of making me do it. She came to me and asked if I thought I could do it." I smirked. "What do you think I said?" I asked her.

She thought for a minute and looked back at me as I opened the door to the café that was attached to the bookstore where my signings were located. "You told her you wanted to, right?" she asked me, so enthusiastically. I could not help but smile.

"Yes, I told her that I wanted to. I wanted to once again prove myself. My parents tried to make me feel like I was different from my brother. I kept thinking that if I could do that, I would finally be worth something to my big brother. So, she handed out the blank white booklets to everyone."

"Then what happened?" she asked.

I place our order and then continue my story. "Imaginations ran wild as everyone in class thought for sure they would win. It was then that I had an idea. You see, I had a crush on this one boy, but so did this other girl who was supposed to be a close friend of mine. I was always the nice one to everyone, but that still didn't get very many people to like me. I knew that if I could win the competition, maybe I could be someone. So, I put him into the book. I wrote my book about a horse that I loved. He was not mine, but he was still special to me. So, I spent all class working on the book. Then I spent days working on the drawings. I am not the best artist, so I decided it would be wise if I stuck to writing. As the week came to an end, we had to hand in our books. I was scared. I thought that I would be the laughingstock of the school."

We grab our drinks, and I leave a couple of dollars in the tip jar. "She took my book and smiled. I knew that I had a chance just like everyone else. I walked back to my desk and sat down. Everyone laughed at me because they thought my story about a horse would be silly and dumb. It crushed me and all my hopes of my book winning. You see, as much as I originally hoped it would impress a boy, once I finished and turned it in, it was different. It was no longer about anyone else but me. I enjoyed the fact that I had discovered a love for writing. I had done something big. Well, big to me, at least. I loved the thought that maybe – just maybe – I really could be good at something."

We took our seats, and I paused. I smiled as I noticed she was practically on the edge of her seat. "Well, the weeks passed, and it was finally time for them to announce the winners. I was terrified that I had messed up somehow. They started with the honorable mentions and went from there. I was so nervous. As they called out the names of some of the top students, I began to lose hope. I had just about given up, but I still clung to a little bit of hope. I knew that I had to listen. I had to know. My teacher was smiling, and everyone was waiting so impatiently."

I take a deep breath as the young teen looks at me as if I were the most interesting thing out there. I could not help but smile at her. "So, who won first place, and what happened next?" she asked. I chuckled.

"Well, you see, I did win. I had won first place. I was so shocked that I looked at the teacher and then back at the speaker and back at her again. I could not believe my ears. 'How is this possible?' I asked. 'I always have such a hard time writing.' The look on the teacher's face was priceless. I do not think she herself even knew. She was simply happy that I had won, and so was I. I asked her if I could go call my mom and tell her, and she let me. I got out of my seat and ran out of the room walked ran straight into the office, still hardly believing what had happened. When I told my mom, she was so excited that I could hear her jumping up and down over the phone."

"I bet you were too. I would be."

"You are right. But then I had to return to class, where all the other students glared at me, upset that I won. My heart hurt and began to wonder if I really deserved it or if I should just reject the prize. I decided no. It wasn't about winning or proving myself anymore. I realized that I would probably never be able to, but it no longer mattered. You see, in school, I might not have been able to spell very, but I was able to write good essays. I loved it and was great at it. That's all that mattered."

She smiled and nodded.

"Soon, we were rushed out of the classroom. As we all went into the lobby, our principle was waiting on us. She congratulated us on everything. She was so proud of us. For once, I was stoked about something that I did amazing on. Come to find out, it was big for the school too. In two weeks, we got to go meet some of the best authors. I was excited. They told me and the rest of the students the reasons they picked my book, and I was beaming with pride. Since then, I have been focused on writing and working with my family. You see, I am not just a writer. I am a professional horse trainer. Some call me a horse whisperer. I also will be going to the NBHA this fall. The point is, you should follow your heart and do the things that you want to do, regardless of what anyone else says. As frustratingly difficult as our issues can become, we can work through them and achieve great things."

"Really? Even me?"

"Of course. To be honest, I was terrified when I wrote my first book, and now it's a big hit. I couldn't be prouder of it. It has helped me overcome almost everything that I knew would hurt me. As the series went on, the sales went through the roof. Oh, boy, my little girl loved the idea of getting more horses for the ranch." I look at her and smile.

She sighs as she looks over at the three kids who bullied her and the table, my heart broke for her. I knew that I had to cheer her up somehow and make her believe in herself and show those other kids what she could do. I knew just how to do that. That would mean coming out telling people bout me. The thought of it turned my stomach. How was I going to manage to get up there and tell everyone my life when I have kept Luna black as in the shadows as I could? No one has ever found out my true identity or where I am from."

I looked at her and took a deep breath. I knew that it was time. "Hey, would you like to go up there with me? I am going to prove to you that we can do this. You and I are a lot alike. There are many reasons why Luna black has stayed in the shadows. I didn't want anyone knowing anything bout me or who I am, but now it's time."

She nods, and I lead her to the table. I introduced her to the others and took a deep breath. I began to wonder if I could do it. *Why did I do that?* I asked myself. *You could have had a smooth book signing, yet here you are, possibly bringing everything you've worked for to an end because some child was crying.*

I shake the thoughts from my mind. I know that everything has to change in life. If I can do this, then maybe she will have the strength to get back out there and follow her dreams. That's all I want for her.

I smile as the crowd cheers as I walk inside. Then I stop short as I hear the other girls yelling at her. I walk right behind her and stand tall, glaring down at them. "May I ask why you are being mean to her?"

They gasp as they spot me. "You're Luna Black, the author," they say in unison. I roll my eyes.

"Yes, but that is that not who I truly am. I am Lucy Bordan. That's right. I am Luna black. I told her to sit here. Now either you go back to your seats, or you can leave," I say through clenched teeth.

Katie walks over and sits her hand down on my shoulder. "Calm down; it's okay. Now, please, let's get on with this signing." I sigh and nod as I turn and hug her. "Thank you so much."

I smile as I look over at my friends and family and my fans. I know that to you the reader and this is just a story. But to me, this is my everyday battle. Many people get bullied and ignored. Either by their parents or classmates. So as the author and a friend I ask that we all stand for each other. Let's bring kindness and love back into the world. We are all the same blood. I have many friends that have been either bullied or the bullier. I helped them all try to be better people. My story holds the truth of my life. It up to you, to find the truth in my story. We are all the same. Let's treat each other the same and be nice.

Remember, there is always some truth behind each story.

From the Author

I started writing when I was in elementary school. I struggled for the most part due to my dyslexia, and people often told me that I would never be a good writer. They told me to give up, but I refused. I gave it everything I had. At one point, I won a young author's award, and I continued writing as I got older. I recently had three short stories published and a fourth accepted for an anthology scheduled for release on March 1st.

My biggest goal with my writing is that others might resonate with my characters and that my stories might empower them in some way and give them the courage to keep going, even when life gets them down. While not all stories have happy endings or see the characters take a positive path, they do typically follow the theme of acceptance -- acceptance of who you are as a person and who you want to be -- and the moment where one decides to stand up for themselves.

CPSIA information can be obtained
at www.ICGtesting.com
Printed in the USA
BVHW071357161120
593415BV00006B/531